THE LEGACY SERIES

SERIES TITLES

Hands
Pardeep Toor

Lafferty, Looking for Love
Dennis McFadden

This Is How We Speak
Rebecca Reynolds

All That It Seems
Jim Landwehr

All Gone Now
Michael Tasker

Your Place in This World
Jake La Botz

I Felt My Life With Both My Hands
Jessica Treadway

Apple & Palm
Patricia Henley

Bodies in Bags
Jamey Gallagher

A Green Glow on the Horizon
Dawn Burns

How We Do Things Here
Matt Cashion

Neon Steel
Jennifer Maritza McCauley

Release of Information
Kali White VanBaale

The Divide
Evan Morgan Williams

Yes, No, I Don't Know
Kathryn Gahl

The Price of Their Toys
John Loonam

The Caged Man
Calvin Mills

A Day Doesn't Go By When I Don't Have Regrets
J. Malcolm Garcia

These Are My People
Steve Fox

We Should Be Somewhere by Now
Stephen Tuttle

Burner and Other Stories
Katrina Denza

The Plan of Chicago
Barry Pearce

Trust Issues
K.P. Davis

Adult Children
Laurence Klavan

Guardians & Saints
Diane Josefowicz

Western Terminus: Stories and A Novella
Michael Keefe

Like Human
Janet Goldberg

The Hopefuls
Elizabeth Oness

Never Stop Exiting
Michael Hopkins

Broken Heart Syndrome
Anne Colwell

The Mexican Messiah: A Novella & Stories
Jay Kauffmann

Close to a Flame
Colleen Alles

American Animism
Jamey Gallagher

Keeping What's Best Left Kept Secret
David Ricchiute

Soaked
Toby LeBlanc

The Path of Totality
Marie Zhuikov

Shocker in Gloomtown
Dan Libman

The Continental Divide
Bob Johnson

The Three Devils and Other Stories
William Luvaas

The Correct Response
Manfred Gabriel

Welcome Back to the World: A Novella & Stories
Rob Davidson

Greyhound Cowboy and Other Stories
Ken Post

Close Call
Kim Suhr

The Waterman
Gary Schanbacher

Signs of the Imminent Apocalypse and Other Stories
Heidi Bell

What We Might Become
Sara Reish Desmond

The Silver State Stories
Michael Darcher

An Instinct for Movement
Michael Mattes

The Machine We Trust
Tim Conrad

Gridlock
Brett Biebel

Salt Folk
Ryan Habermeyer

The Commission of Inquiry
Patrick Nevins

Maximum Speed
Kevin Clouther

Reach Her in This Light
Jane Curtis

The Spirit in My Shoes
John Michael Cummings

The Effects of Urban Renewal on Mid-Century America and Other Crime Stories
Jeff Esterholm

What Makes You Think You're Supposed to Feel Better
Jody Hobbs Hesler

Fugitive Daydreams
Leah McCormack

Hoist House: A Novella & Stories
Jenny Robertson

Finding the Bones: Stories & A Novella
Nikki Kallioy

Self-Defense
Corey Mertes

Where Are Your People From?
James B. De Monte

Sometimes Creek
Steve Fox

The Plagues
Joe Baumann

The Clayfields
Elise Gregory

Kind of Blue
Christopher Chambers

Evangelina Everyday
Dawn Burns

Township
Jamie Lyn Smith

Responsible Adults
Patricia Ann McNair

Great Escapes from Detroit
Joseph O'Malley

Nothing to Lose
Kim Suhr

The Appointed Hour
Susanne Davis

PRAISE FOR
HANDS

In this brilliant new collection, Toor ignites the page with his wit and heart. He has the range and precise ability to make you laugh even as it stings. He navigates growth, family, immigration, and desire like a practiced craftsman. This is a beautiful work of art.

—NANA KWAME ADJEI-BRENYAH
National Book Award Finalist
author of *Chain-Gang All-Stars* and *Friday Black*

I'm struck by how beautifully crafted, resonant, and remarkable these stories are. There is a sense of hope and honesty evident here that is both profoundly moving and essential to understanding the human condition. Pardeep Toor is an exciting, bold new writer with endless talent.

—BRANDON HOBSON
National Book Award Finalist
author of *The Devil is a Southpaw*

A critique of the American Dream, labor, and class. In *Hands*, Toor writes sharply and movingly about a high school dropout, a brown man with a heavy Indian accent, as he begins to find the limitations that await him in Michigan. You won't envy these characters for a second, but you will come to understand the ensnarled conditions they cannot escape as working-class immigrants. Seedy at times, hilarious, and deeply engrossing, this is an unforgettable collection.

—ANNA QU
author of *Made In China*

Hands is as devastating, hilarious, and absurd as the immigrant experience itself. A must-read for anyone who has felt out of place in the world, no matter where they were born.

—MARIA KUZNETSOVA
author of *Oksana, Behave!*

HANDS

stories

PARDEEP TOOR

CORNERSTONE PRESS
UNIVERSITY OF WISCONSIN-STEVENS POINT

Cornerstone Press, Stevens Point, Wisconsin 54481
Copyright © 2026 Pardeep Toor
www.uwsp.edu/cornerstone

Printed in the United States of America.

ISBN: 978-1-968148-36-2

All rights reserved.

This is a work of fiction. Names, characters, businesses, places, events, and incidents are either the products of the author's imagination or used in a fictitious manner. Any resemblance to actual persons, living or dead, or actual events is purely coincidental.

Cornerstone Press titles are produced in courses and internships offered by the Department of English at the University of Wisconsin–Stevens Point.

DIRECTOR & PUBLISHER	EXECUTIVE EDITORS
Dr. Ross K. Tangedal	Jeff Snowbarger, Freesia McKee
EDITORIAL DIRECTOR	SENIOR EDITORS
Brett Hill	Lhea Owens, Paige Biever

PRESS STAFF
Samantha Bjork, Sophie McPherson, Eleanor Belcher, Kim Janesch, Brianna Loving, Oliver McKnight, Hannah Rouer, Sam Zajkowski, Andrew Bryant

For Milo and Rio – My Dreams Come True

STORIES

Gatsby   1

Taxi   14

Stranded in the Dunes   24

Dinner Party   40

Tony and Jim's   59

The Astrologer   78

Acknowledgments   95

I stayed in the library, crushed breathless by the smoldering power of all those words—many of them unfathomable—until Happy Hour. And then I left.

The motor traffic was relentless, the sidewalks were crowded, the people were preoccupied and mean, because Happy Hour was also Rush Hour.

During Happy Hour, when you pay for one drink, he gives you two.

Happy Hour lasts two hours.

—Denis Johnson, "Happy Hour"

GATSBY

Hans suspected they preyed on him because of his skin color. "It's because we're brown," he said, in the cafeteria line. "That's why they hurt us."

"Real men fight back," Kanti said. "That's the rule in this country."

Hans trusted Kanti knew the traditions better than he did. Kanti had come to Michigan before Hans. He was the first Indian at their high school. Hans was the second. They were the darkest students at school, took the same classes, shared a locker, and ate lunch together every day. Hans relied on Kanti for help with his homework and the unwritten rules of high school. Without Kanti, Hans wouldn't have known that he couldn't smoke cigarettes in the hallway, talk to girls who wore cross necklaces—no matter how nice they seemed—or sit in the back of the classroom with the jocks or in the front with the serious students. The middle was invisible in America.

"Fighting doesn't solve anything," Hans said. He sat across from Kanti in a corner of the cafeteria, between the Coca-Cola and Hershey's vending machines. The school was full of farmers. Boys tucked their Dickies shirts into their carpenter jeans and wore John Deere hats. Girls tugged at their knee-length floral dresses and tied their hair tightly in buns.

Hans told his classmates that he was a farmer too. His family owned land in a small village in northwest India, close to the Pakistan border. They were connected by agriculture and bonded by knowledge of dairy, wheat, and corn. But Hans didn't own land in Michigan, so according to his classmates, it didn't matter what he had left back home.

"What would you do if you were me?" Hans said.

"I wouldn't have looked at Steve's girlfriend," Kanti said.

"Everyone looks at the cheerleaders, even the teachers."

"I like their miniskirts too."

Hans poked his cold breadsticks with a plastic fork, jealous of the hot dogs and hamburgers on other plates. His sister, Aarti, took him to an astrologer who advised against eating meat if he wanted success in his new country. Hans could use any help he could get. "They're nice to look at," he said.

"Steve is your problem now, not her," Kanti said. "You have to fight him."

Steve was a popular football player. He played a position that never touched the ball but tackled others on every play. Kanti said Steve was good. Hans couldn't tell the difference between Steve and the other players. He only saw overweight boys hitting each other until the referee blew the whistle. The ball would appear from underneath the pile of bodies. Then half the team would run to the sideline and a new group did it again.

"Will you help me?" Hans said.

"Only bad guys ask for interference," Kanti said.

"But we're the good guys."

"Then why is Steve hunting you?"

"I didn't do anything."

"Come over this afternoon and we'll practice."

"Practice what?"

"Wrestling," Kanti said. "I have some tapes of Gorgeous George that will help you."

"How is TV wrestling going to help me?" Hans said.

"I'll be waiting out front." Kanti threw an empty Skittles wrapper on his tray and left the table.

The cafeteria was nearly empty. Most students, including Steve, had traveled to the neighboring county for an afternoon meet, where boys and girls in tiny shorts ran a few kilometers only to end up where they started. Steve had promised to hurt Hans after the meet because Hans had "looked at his girlfriend funny." Hans didn't understand why everything was funny in this country. His skin darkened in the spring. That was hilarious. He got pushed into a locker while changing for gym class and his classmates erupted in laughter. They wrote "Paki" on his locker with red lipstick, even though he was from India, not Pakistan. "Funny" was fuel for the American mob.

Hans accidentally bumped into a few classmates in the hallway illuminated with faint tube lights and the dull shine of cinderblocks. Most students wore school colors on Fridays. Hans didn't have enough money to purchase the gray hoodie with the red emblem of a knight's helmet. He still relied on his hand-sewn khaki pants and knitted sweaters from back home. The loose clothing hid his scrawny frame, which could help him escape Steve's grip.

A voice called to him from the end of the hallway. "Look over here."

Jessica wore a glittery red cheerleader skirt. Her legs were thin but muscular. A gold necklace hung around her neck and crept into the V-neck of her tank top. There was probably a cross hidden in her chest.

"You just did it again," she said.

"Did what?" Hans said.

"Looked at me funny."

"I didn't see anything."

"But you tried."

"I have to go," Hans said. He tried passing her, but she stepped in front of him.

"You shady people come here and think you can take everything from us."

"I don't need anything from you."

"You just did it again. You can't do that."

"Did what?"

"Tried to see through my clothes."

"You're barely wearing any clothes," Hans said.

"I'm glad Steve is going to kill you after school," Jessica said.

Why did they want to hurt him? What was he supposed to do, walk around school with his head down? Then they would say it was strange that he didn't look up while walking or make eye contact with others. "I'm a good guy," Hans said.

Jessica took a step back. "You're dead meat, Hands."

Hans headed for the exit, past lockers decorated with violent monikers calling to "destroy" and "kill" students from the rival school. Violence was an obsession. Each neighboring county in Michigan was like an India versus Pakistan skirmish. They had their own flags, police forces, and hunting lands.

Hans pulled the door handle of the yellow taxi at the roundabout reserved for school buses. It was locked.

"What's the magic word?" Kanti said, from the driver's seat.

"Nobody understands that stupid book."

Kanti lit a cigarette.

"Gatsby," Hans said.

The lock opened with a loud, echoing click.

"Show me the wrestling tapes," Hans said.

"What's gotten into you?" Kanti said, finishing his cigarette while pulling out of the school.

"We deserve to be here as much as they do."

"Who's kicking us out?"

"Jessica said I deserve to die."

"Did you look at her again?"

"Why can't we look?"

"This is a free country," Kanti said. "You can look wherever you want."

Hans hoped to channel his anger into a winning strategy to beat Steve. He wanted Jessica to watch. They always underestimated him and assumed he would run away. This time he would fight back.

"It's not fair," Hans said. "These girls throw themselves at guys like Steve and won't let us even look."

Kanti leaned over to open the glove compartment. He pulled out a gun. "This is also an option."

"Put that away," Hans said, startled.

"It's my dad's revolver. He keeps it for protection."

"Does it work?"

"My dad said it killed three Pakistanis back home."

"We can't kill Steve."

At a stoplight, Kanti rolled down his window and pointed the gun toward the sky. "One look at this thing will scare him off."

"Don't shoot," Hans said.

"Watch this." Kanti stuck his head out the window. The car drifted into the intersection as his foot slipped off the brake.

"Get back in the car," Hans said. He covered his ears as multiple loud clicks rang in the empty intersection.

"You're a chicken," Kanti said, laughing. He released the empty cylinder and shoved it in Hans's face. "It's not loaded."

Hans grabbed the gun and threw it into the glove compartment. "We're not murderers."

"You know we can leave all this," Kanti said.

"We're not killing anybody," Hans said.

"My dad wants me to take over the taxi full-time, day and night."

"What's he going to do?"

"Government contracts for trash pickup."

"There's money in garbage?"

"The real money is in transporting stuff, not people."

"What about school?"

"School isn't for people like us."

"Because we're the dark ones here?"

"Because we're here to make money."

"How much money?" Hans said.

"Big money," Kanti said. "Day shift is yours. Nights are mine."

The thought of a job momentarily numbed Hans's anger. The money would be nice. He could finally stop eating the free cold meals at the cafeteria and go across the street to Tony and Jim's, the local pizzeria that sold by the slice.

"Are the taxi customers dangerous?" Hans said.

"You're not safe at school either," Kanti said

They pulled into Kanti's house, a tiny two-story cube. The gutters above the rusty side panels leaked. Fall leaves smothered the cracked driveway. Soon, snow would suffocate the grass, and Diwali would again be overshadowed by Thanksgiving. His classmates would trade in pencils and jeans for hunting rifles and camo, and Hans would be in remedial classes after another failed semester. The new year would arrive with the same challenges at school.

Hans followed Kanti to the unfinished basement. The furnace hummed amidst open boxes and old furniture. A television with a built-in VCR sat on a lawn chair. The plaid couch facing the television was missing a middle cushion.

"The wrestling tapes are in one of these boxes," Kanti said.

Hans sifted through a box of turmeric-stained plastic containers, expired bulk bags of lentils and rice, and half-burnt candles. "You really think this is going to work?"

"The first step is thinking like a wrestler," Kanti said.

"Steve doesn't want to wrestle. He wants to kill me."

"Why do you think Steve is so strong?"

"Because he plays sports?"

"Because he watches wrestling."

"You don't know anything," Hans said.

"Steve is in your head," Kanti said. "Gorgeous George invented ring psychology. He's the only one who can help you now."

Maybe it would be more productive for Hans to lift weights or ride the stationary bike in the basement than watch videos of half-naked men grabbing one another. He needed to get stronger and faster quickly.

Kanti handed Hans a box. "Take this one. You'll like what's in there."

The couch springs squeaked when Hans sat down. He opened the box. There were issues of *Playboy* magazine inside. The woman on the cover crossed her arms over her naked body and clenched her thighs together. Her creamy white skin shined without blemish. Her green eyes dared Hans to keep staring. Her long dark hair led his gaze to parts of her that excited him. The sudden urge was uncontrollable, like when he looked at girls in the school hallway or the cheerleaders practicing on the fields.

"Those are my dad's magazines," Kanti said. "He's always down here looking at them."

Hans held up the magazine. "She's beautiful."

"Wait until you see what's inside."

Hans flipped through the magazine. The woman's arms and legs were spread open in the pictures. Imagination was irrelevant when he could already see everything. Her nakedness appeared normal, like it was her natural state. This was the freedom Hans had fantasized about and expected in America. Not school and fights.

Kanti stood beside Hans. "The things I'd do to her if she was in my taxi," he said, twirling his hands in his pockets.

"What would you do?" Hans said.

"All kinds of things."

"Name one."

"Touch her all over."

"Even here?" Hans said, pointing to her exposed midsection.
"Especially there," Kanti said. "I'd start there."
"What else?"
"You know what else. I don't have to tell you."
"Tell me."
"Come on. You already know."

In one picture the woman wore a cowboy hat and boots and held a rifle, then was draped in a yellow flag with an image of a snake, and in another one she only wore a crown. Her wavy brown hair flowed freely in all the pictures. Hans desired to study her poses and agonize over her every word in the article next to the pictures. Where was her favorite place to eat? What type of music did she like? Where did she live? He could accommodate all her needs in the taxi. He would never tire of looking at her in the rearview mirror.

The static blur of the television seized Hans's attention. He dropped the magazine. It lay open on a picture of the woman lying on a leopard print rug.

Kanti rewound and forwarded the tape until he reached Gorgeous George's entrance. "Pay attention to how he enters the ring. His presence is everything."

"He's wearing ostrich feathers," Hans said.
"They intimidate his opponents."
"Steve won't be scared of bird feathers."
"Just watch."

Gorgeous George plucked and tossed feathers into the crowd while circling his opponent in the ring, condescendingly pointing at his bald head, large ears, and rolls of stomach fat. Upon the referee's pleading, Gorgeous George finally disrobed to reveal his high-waisted tights and muscular chest. He gazed into the camera, straightened his back, adjusted his broad shoulders, and laughed at the crowd.

Kanti slouched on the sofa and planted his hands in his pants. "Who do you think has a bigger chest—Gorgeous George or the girl in the magazine?"

"How will this help me fight Steve?" Hans said.

"Keep watching," Kanti said.

Gorgeous George's opponent was a darker brute, somewhere between brown and black.

The announcer called him "Samoan." The crowd stirred as he arrogantly stomped around the ring and barbarically lunged at George. The announcer declared, "He's jealous of Gorgeous George's pure beauty."

"He's wearing makeup," Hans said.

"It brings out his eyes," Kanti said. "Makes him look dangerous."

"He looks like our English teacher, the blonde one who wears tight skirts."

"Gorgeous George is a real man."

"This is nonsense."

"Watch his moves," Kanti said. "He's quick, goes for the ankles, and snaps the other guy's leg."

Gorgeous George spent the first part of the match hugging the ropes to escape submission holds. He flailed out of an arm bar, front chin lock, and head scissors chokehold. Once upright, he readjusted his blond locks and pranced around the ring.

"My fight with Steve is real," Hans said.

"Look how real Gorgeous George's muscles are."

"This isn't helping."

Kanti dug his hands deeper into his pants. "Let's finish this match. Then we'll go back to school."

Hans watched closely. Gorgeous George circled his opponent and kept him guessing. His attacks were sparse and erratic. When he got hold of a limb, he didn't let go. He kept twisting and turning, applying his force on joints and bones. Maybe Hans could wear Steve out with his speed and circle him until he got dizzy. Then his wobbling legs would be vulnerable to an attack. One jolt to the back of his knee would stagger him. Another charge to the opposite knee would bring him down. From there, Hans could wrap his arms around Steve's neck in a sleeper hold. It would hurt and humiliate him in front of Jessica and the entire school.

"You really think I have a shot against Steve?" Hans said.

"Make sure you swing your arms like Gorgeous George when you walk toward him," Kanti said. "Let me show you."

Kanti marched back and forth between the television. "Wrestling is all about confidence." He grabbed Hans's arm and twisted it behind his back.

"Get off me," Hans said.

"How will you fight Steve if you can't even handle me?"

Furious, Hans stretched until Kanti's grip on him loosened. They faced each other.

"We wrestle for it," Kanti said. "I win and you join my taxi business."

"And if I win, you help me beat Steve," Hans said, ducking and tackling Kanti by his ankles. Kanti tried kicking out of his grip, but Hans planted his foot on Kanti's back to anchor him to the floor.

"This isn't wrestling," Kanti said.

Hans pulled Kanti's arms behind his back until his shoulders cracked. "Do you give up?"

"You haven't pinned me yet," Kanti said.

Hans let go of Kanti's arms, fell to his knees, rolled Kanti onto his back, and pinned his wrists to the ground over his head. "Surrender," he said.

"My shoulders are still up."

Hans swung a leg over Kanti and bounced on his midsection, knocking the wind out of him.

Kanti groaned and shook his head. "I quit," he said.

Hans fell off Kanti. With Kanti's help, he would have a real chance to beat Steve. "Do you think Jessica gets naked for Steve like the girl in the magazine?" Hans said, panting.

"After every football game, I bet," Kanti said, between desperate breaths. "You hurt my shoulder."

"Do you think she'll do it for me if I beat him up?"

"You'll have to kill him first."

Hans rolled up the *Playboy* and stuffed it into his pocket. "Let's get this over with," he said.

"After Gorgeous George," Kanti said. "It's almost over."

"Now," Hans said as he walked up the stairs.

Outside, a few more leaves had fallen onto the hood of the taxi. Hans carefully lifted the wipers and plucked twigs off the windshield. He circled the taxi. A few scratches, but overall, it was in good condition. Transportation work could be good for him, if his sister and the astrologer approved. It wouldn't keep him in one place for too long. People like Steve would need him for brief stretches, from one location to another, so they wouldn't bother to pick a fight. The taxi would finally make him visible to others.

Was this why he'd come to America? So he could cart others around like a *rickshaw* driver? He could've done that in India. Wasn't he supposed to get a real job, one that involved reading and required nice pants and shirts? He could dress nicely in the taxi too. That would attract more customers. Then one day he could upgrade the taxi into a limo, then two or three limos, and finally a driving school to train future taxi and limo drivers. Would that be enough, or would he have to keep fighting for more?

Kanti rushed out the door with keys in hand and a cigarette dangling between his lips. "Gorgeous George pulled a hammer from under the ring when the referee wasn't looking and knocked the dark guy out," Kanti said. "George won. You have a chance too."

Hans inspected the interior of the taxi. The heat worked well, and the radio dial was smooth and easy to navigate. The cigarette smell could be aired out over time. Plastic mats would be necessary for the winter months.

"Tell me how this will work," Hans said.

"First you delay by circling around Steve," Kanti said.

"I mean the taxi."

"The money is going to be big."

Hans opened the glove compartment and wrapped the gun in the magazine. "And what about the girls?"

"Money makes anything possible in America," Kanti said.

The taxi's brakes squeaked as they pulled into the school. The buses were back from the running meet. The crowd turned toward the parking lot, with Steve's lumbering figure in the center. It was impossible to hide a yellow taxi with the only two brown kids in school.

"Did I really hurt your shoulder?" Hans said.

"I won't be much help to you now," Kanti said.

The menacing mob fell behind Steve and marched in their direction. They snarled at Hans with the same intensity as they probably had versus their rival earlier that afternoon. They desired more violence, rushed to inflict greater pain, and searched for an even bigger victory. No teachers were in sight to stop them.

"What's our plan?" Kanti said.

Hans sized up Steve. His blond hair perfectly matched his pale skin. The school shirt exaggerated his muscles, as if tailored for his body. It made sense that girls liked Steve. He was fifty yards away, then forty. He crossed the grass and stepped onto the asphalt, thirty yards away from the taxi.

Hans took the gun from the glove compartment. It was heavy in his hands, like the textbooks he never learned to read.

Kanti took the gun and loaded the cylinder with bullets. "Aim for his head," he said.

Hans thought about the first day of hunting season in Michigan, when hallways and classrooms emptied. Kanti said their classmates woke up before sunrise, bathed in strange soaps, wore military clothes, loaded their guns, and hid in trees at the county park waiting for deer. Even teachers were more interested in dead deer on those days than classes.

"Or maybe fire a warning shot into the sky like Hollywood movies?" Kanti said.

Animals were treated differently back home. They helped with chores on the farm and contributed to daily meals. They were nurtured, not hunted. Hans had never hurt any of them. But Hans knew his classmates were killers. They brought deer for lunch to prove it. He was just another dark target for them to conquer, and they wouldn't stop until he was dead meat.

"It's time," Kanti said.

Escape was an option. Taxi life could exist between these conflicts, transporting Hans between hunter and prey. Or he could fight back against Steve right now.

Hans got out of the taxi with the gun. Kanti locked the door.

"That's not funny," Hans said.

"Remember Gorgeous George," Kanti said.

"Unlock the door."

"We're here to end this."

Hans slapped the car window. "Open the door," he said. His wrist trembled as he pointed the gun at Steve. The stock was drenched with sweat from his palm.

Kanti pointed at the crowd through the windshield. "Their heads."

Hans continued banging on the car window. "Gatsby," he said. "Gatsby!" Steve and the crowd crept closer, undisturbed by the gun in Hans's hand.

Had Hans exhausted all options? He believed he had. A clicking noise echoed loudly in the school parking lot.

TAXI

Hans parked the yellow cab in front of a lime-green house near the central part of the city, amid the cheaply constructed square municipal buildings. He fumbled with the lever to adjust the seat. He pushed forward, backward, and then forward again until he felt comfortable with the space between his knees and the steering wheel. He put both his hands on the steering wheel and pretended to drive.

Hans didn't own the cab. He had borrowed it from Kanti. Kanti's dad made him drop out of high school to start driving the yellow cab. Hans drove the cab during weekday mornings and afternoons. Kanti preferred nights and weekends when business was best. Kanti left the car in the school parking lot every morning before teachers, secretaries, or anyone who could recognize him arrived. He left the keys under the driver's seat mat. Hans didn't read well enough to understand the stories in English class or the math problems in algebra. He was too weak for gym class. He preferred to drive the taxi.

Hans looked at the house. There were two large windows on either side of the door. A red light shined through the holes in the brown curtain on one of the windows. Cracks in the other window resembled a spider's web. The front door opened. The windows shook when it slammed shut. A woman stepped out of the house clutching a young boy by the hood of his navy-blue bubble jacket. She pulled the hood for balance. The boy's head jerked back in her grasp with each step but his eyes remained focused on the icy asphalt in front of them. She hesitated down the stairs, especially the bottom wooden plank that was propped up with crumbling bricks. The path from their front door to the cab was muddled with slush and small piles of dirty snow.

The woman fell into the cab as she reached for the door. She pulled the handle. The door didn't open. Hans's shoulder cracked when he reached for the lock. The woman slapped the rear window. Hans lifted the lock up. The woman pulled the door open and stepped back a few steps. The boy ducked and spun in a circle to free himself from the woman.

"Get over here," the woman said. The boy's tiny hand grazed the hood of the cab as he ran to the passenger side door. He wasn't tall enough to reach the window, so he knocked on the door.

"Open up, mister," the boy said.

Hans unlocked the door. The boy jumped into the car.

"Get in the back with me," the woman said.

The woman struggled to place herself in the backseat. She dove into the car headfirst. Her baseball cap fell as she sprawled across the seat on her stomach before dragging her feet in. She pushed herself up off the seat. She adjusted her bleached jeans at the knees before sitting upright. She put her hat back on. Her stringy hair protruded from the rim of the hat and matted her bangs over her forehead.

"I'm fine up here, Mom. Mister doesn't mind," the boy said.

"I don't mind," Hans said.

The woman reached over the front passenger seat to buckle her son's seatbelt. Her eyes were red, and an odorous cloud engulfed Hans with familiarity and disgust. The odor, her unsteady hand, anxious fingers, and scars on her cheeks evoked nostalgia in Hans.

"Where can I take you on this wonderful Tuesday morning?" Hans said, in accordance with the script Kanti provided him. He made eye contact with the woman through the rearview mirror.

"Where do you want to go?" the woman said, poking the boy in the arm.

"Burger World," he said.

"Not Burger World," she said. "Let's go to Joe's Tacos."

"But I want Burger World."

"But Mom wants tacos so we're going to Joe's," the woman said.

Hans glanced at the boy and then the woman.

"So?" Hans said.

"You do what I say and I say Joe's," the woman said.

Hans looked at the boy one more time.

"Why are you looking at him? I'm the one paying you."

"I'm sorry, ma'am," Hans said.

Hans started the meter and shifted the car into drive. The boy pulled out a plastic handheld game from his jacket pocket, a maze with a small silver marble inside. He gently maneuvered his hands to guide the marble to the hole in the center.

Hans stopped at a red light.

"Can I smoke in the car?" the woman said.

"No problem," Hans said.

Hans had smoked his last cigarette the previous summer on a riverbank, about twenty miles west of the city. Kanti took him there for a vacation day. They smoked together with their feet in the cold river water. Even in the summer, the river was cold. Hans remembered the taste in his mouth from the last cigarette. He had accidentally put the lit side in his mouth. The butt left a permanent burn mark on the inside of his lips. It was the last time he had smoked or visited the river.

Hans turned to the boy, who didn't look up from his pocket game.

"Do you have a light?" the woman said.

Hans pretended to check his pockets. He opened the glove compartment in front of the boy's feet and tried to quickly close it before the gun fell out. A book dropped on the boy's feet. The boy picked it up. On the cover was an illustration of a man and a woman, their bodies entangled. The title of the book was *Pleasurable Positions*. Hans grabbed the book and put it under his thigh. Hans looked back at the woman. She kicked Hans's seat while shuffling her legs side-to-side. Hans searched the compartment underneath the radio but couldn't find a lighter.

"I don't have one," Hans said. "I don't smoke anymore."

"Why did you stop smoking?" the boy said.

"Health reasons," Hans said.

"There's nothing wrong with my health," the woman said.

The boy put the handheld game in his pocket and wiped his nose with his jacket sleeve. His shirt was too small for him. His wrists were exposed to the cold. His pants were stained with mud at the knees and around the ankles. Hans turned the heat up.

"Pull over here at Mario's store. I need a lighter," the woman said.

"Where?"

"Mario's. Right here. You're passing it. Turn," the woman said.

The car slid on the ice as Hans stopped in the middle turning lane. He looked in both directions but didn't see Mario's. Cars honked at him from both directions.

"Mario's is on the next block, Mom," the boy said. "Keep going, mister."

The woman leaned forward in her seat. She placed a cigarette in her mouth and twirled another one in her fingers. "Don't you dare talk to me like that again," she said.

"I didn't say anything," the boy said.

"Like that. Just like that. Don't do it."

Hans inhaled the anticipated stench from the burning cigarette. He swallowed his built-up saliva and began to whistle in the car to mimic the act of blowing smoke through his lips. He merged with traffic and drove slowly to the next block.

"Did you use the patch, mister?" the boy said.

"What?" Hans said.

"The cigarette patch. To quit smoking."

"No, I quit on my own," Hans said. "My sister helped me. She rubbed my legs with oils all night when I was in withdrawal."

"Why doesn't your sister help us, Mom?" the boy said.

"We don't need anyone's help," she said.

"They might have a lighter over there," Hans said. He pointed to a store at the corner of the next intersection. The building's white side panels were stained with streaks of rust from the leaky gutters. A small handwritten sign in the window said DOLLAR PALACE.

"That's Mario's," the woman said.

"It says Dollar Palace," Hans said.

"It's Mario's," the boy said.

The woman opened the car door before Hans finished parking and stepped into a puddle. She knocked on Hans's window. He rolled it down.

"Do you want something? A bag of chips?" she said.

"No, thank you," Hans said. Kanti had instructed him to never accept anything from customers.

"Can I get a bag of chips?" the boy said.

"Do you have any money?"

"No," the boy said.

"Then the answer is no."

"The meter is running," Hans called after the woman as she walked away from the car.

Hans looked at the boy. The boy stared back.

"What's in that book?" the boy said.

"What book?"

"The one under your leg."

"It's not mine. It's my partner Kanti's."

"What's in it?"
"I don't know," Hans said.
"Is it sex?"
Hans shrugged.
"My brother told me about that stuff," the boy said.
"I haven't read it," Hans said.
"You're lying."
"How do you know?" Hans said.
"My mom is a liar. I know liars."
Hans reached into his pocket and pulled out a dollar bill. "Here, go get yourself a bag of chips."
The boy took the dollar and opened the door. He threw his jacket on the seat and sprinted into Mario's. Hans felt sorry for the boy. He was a child. He was hungry. Hans hit the buttons on the meter to try to stop the red analog numbers from ticking up but the meter couldn't be paused. Hans turned on the radio, scanned the stations, and then turned it off. Feeling claustrophobic, he rolled down his window, stuck his head out, and took a deep breath. The wind stung his gums and cheeks. The cab smelled like cigarette smoke. He searched for an air freshener under the seat but couldn't find one. He scanned the cover of the book and then put it back in the glove compartment. Hans rested his head on his window and tapped his feet to the music that was no longer playing. The salt and slush under his shoes swished from one side of the mat to the other. The door to Mario's opened and closed several times but the woman and boy were nowhere to be seen. He saw more people exit Mario's than he'd seen enter.
Hans lifted the boy's jacket off the seat. It reeked of smoke. He put it down. He picked it up again. He closed his eyes and looked away from the jacket as he squeezed it in his hand. The fabric made a squishing noise in his fist. He looked at the door to Mario's again. He lowered himself in his seat and pulled the jacket to his face. Hans inhaled the burnt smoky

smell. He swirled his tongue on the inner fleece lining of the jacket. The putrid smell and taste of the fabric invigorated him, like a cup of coffee in the morning.

Hans's chest shook. He sat up and saw the door to Mario's open. The woman and the boy were yelling at each other. Each carried a small bag of chips. Hans stuffed the jacket in the glove compartment on top of the sex book.

The woman and the boy got back into the car. "Off to Burger World now," the woman said.

Hans waited for their doors to close. "I thought we were going to Joe's Tacos," he said.

"I want Burger World," the woman said. She held a cigarette in her lips and rolled down her window.

"You said Joe's before," the boy said.

"What did I tell you about talking back to me?"

"You said Joe's."

"I said Burger World," the woman said.

"Burger World then?" Hans said.

"I guess," the boy said.

The woman shifted forward to the edge of the seat until she was face-to-face with the boy. She grabbed the front of the boy's shirt. "I warned you about this," she said. "I warned you about talking so much." She let go of his shirt and slapped his chest softly three times.

"Turn this car around right now," the woman said. "We're going home."

"Mom, I didn't say anything," the boy said.

Hans looked down to see a cigarette in the cupholder between the two front seats. It must have fallen out of her mouth.

"We're going home," she said.

"Mom, please."

"Home."

Hans put the car in drive and headed toward the lime-green house. The boy put his head in his hands.

"Don't cry," the woman said.
"I'm not crying."
"I didn't teach you to cry."
"You always do this."
"Do what?" the woman said. "What am I doing?"
"Nothing," the boy said.
"That's what I thought."

They drove the rest of the way in silence. Hans sped up at yellow lights and rolled through stop signs. He parked in front of the house and stopped the meter.

"I didn't tell you to stop that meter," the woman said.
"We're home," Hans said.
"You wait here. Keep that meter going."

The woman and the boy exited the car and silently walked into the house. Hans gently picked up the cigarette from the cupholder. He was careful not to squeeze it between his thumb and index finger. The integrity of the shape was important. He examined it carefully from all angles. He sniffed it from one side to the other. He placed it in the glove compartment, beside the boy's jacket. He licked his thumb and index finger. The taste of tobacco made him salivate. The woman and boy stepped out of the house. They both got in the backseat this time.

Hans looked at himself in the rearview mirror. His cheeks were red. Flakes of dry skin smothered his chin.

"We decided on Waffle Place," the woman said.
"I'm getting the Mega Meal," the boy said.

Hans began driving toward Waffle Place. It was on the other side of town, in the opposite direction of Joe's Tacos and Burger World.

Hans looked in the rearview mirror. The woman and the boy were cuddled up together. The boy smiled each time the woman tickled his arm. Hans turned on the radio. The boy stood in his seat and started dancing to the song.

"Put your seatbelt on," the woman said. She pulled the boy closer and sat him down in the seat. She buckled the middle seatbelt around his waist and put her arms around his shoulders. Her fingers tapped his elbow to the rhythm of the song.

Hans stopped at a red light, two blocks short of Waffle Place. "Are you okay with the temperature?" he said.

"I'm cold," the boy said.

Hans directed the vents toward them and turned up the heat.

"It will take a minute," Hans said.

"Where's your jacket?" the woman said.

The boy clutched his arms. "I don't know," he said.

The woman leaned forward and felt around the front seat.

"What's wrong?" Hans said.

"Have you seen his jacket?" the woman said.

"What color was it?"

The woman turned to the boy. "Answer the man."

"Blue," the boy said.

"Are you sure you brought it in the cab?" Hans said.

"It's my favorite jacket," the boy said.

The woman looked around the backseat. "It's not here," she said. "Stand up."

The boy struggled with the seatbelt. The woman grabbed it from his hands and unbuckled it.

"You hurt my hand," the boy said.

"Maybe you left it at the house?" Hans said.

"Stand up," the woman said.

The boy stood in the seat, curving his neck to avoid the ceiling of the car. He stumbled forward in his seat when Hans stopped at the light.

"Where's the jacket?" the woman said.

"I don't know," the boy said.

Hans reached for the meter on the dashboard. He nudged the glove compartment closed again.

"We're here," Hans said.
"Who told you to turn the meter off?" the woman said. "Turn it on."
"Why?" Hans said.
"Start it again. We're going home."
"I want Waffle Place," the boy said.
"You're not getting anything until we find your jacket."

Hans circled the parking lot and turned back toward the lime-green house. He looked in the rearview mirror. The woman was mumbling to herself, loud enough for the boy to hear. The boy was crying. He made eye contact with Hans through the mirror. Hans focused on the road ahead. The boy stared at Hans every time he glanced at the rearview mirror.

"Drive faster. Stop milking the meter," the woman said.

Hans drove faster. He needed the jacket more than the boy needed waffles. Hans hoped one day the boy would understand.

STRANDED IN THE DUNES

Hans was reading the same page of his real estate book for the seventh time when a rock smashed through his bedroom window. Fragments of glass scattered across his mattress on the floor.

Two bright headlights penetrated the broken window and flashed against the bare off-white walls of his room. Outside, Kanti stood beside his yellow cab. He waved his hands at Hans, guiding him outside as an air traffic controller would wave in a plane.

Hans felt a sharp pain in his back when he picked up yesterday's pants and shirt from the floor and shook them to release the window shards caught in the wrinkles and pockets. The pain bounced around like a marble crashing against a glass jar. Each movement was another collision. At some point, either the glass or marble had to shatter.

Hans hoped the clothes would be warm enough to overcome the morning chill that now stormed into his bedroom. Kanti had made another mess for him to clean up. Hans vowed to make him pay for the damage.

A pile of cigarette ashes overflowed in the disconnected plastic smoke detector on the bathroom counter. Hans bent over the sink and twisted his head until he wrapped his mouth completely around the faucet. He turned on the cold water and let it pool in his cheeks before swallowing. He wanted to splash his face, maybe brush his teeth, but Kanti blasted the car horn outside.

"I'm coming," Hans said, slipping the real estate book into his pocket.

Kanti had removed the taxi sign from the top of the car and was warming his hands against the heating vents with an open beer between his legs.

Hans blew into his frigid hands. "You're paying for that broken window."

"Relax, it was probably broken before," Kanti said.

"I am relaxed."

"No, really relax," Kanti said.

"You don't know what it's like to study all night," Hans said.

"We quit school a long time ago."

"This is something else."

"What else?"

Every night before bed, Hans promised himself that tomorrow he'd begin planning to realize his dreams. He made a mental checklist of everything he needed to do in the morning to get started. But something always got in the way. Too many drinks, or the taxi shift, but usually it was Kanti. Hans mounted the accumulated pressure of incomplete dreams on his head, like a tightly tied turban.

Lately, Hans dreamed about becoming a realtor. One of his taxi fares had left the book in the cab. At first, Hans didn't think much of it. He kept it in the glove compartment for a few days, waiting for the customer to reclaim it. The call never came so he began reading it between rides. Zoning, commercial versus residential, floor plans, square footage—all valuable concepts in his new profession. There were good locations and bad locations. Every property was an opportunity for profit. Hans wouldn't need Kanti or his taxi after he got his realtor's license. He would sell properties and make new friends who wore nice sweaters and pleated pants—friends who drank coffee and agonized about the weather forecast every morning. Hans would find a nice girl after he became a professional realtor, one who wore flowery summer dresses that matched her straw hats, cooked pasta, and served a salad with every meal.

"We're going to find you a girl at the lake," Kanti said.

"What do you know about getting girls?" Hans said.

"Do you remember Jessica?"

"Steve's girlfriend?"

"I had some fun with her," Kanti said.

Hans knew Kanti was lying, but his lies were harmless. They exaggerated his accomplishments to a degree that made him sound ridiculous.

"A girl will help you relax," Kanti said.

Hans closed his eyes and recalled the plan they'd made earlier in the week. Kanti had just gotten back from a day-long taxi ride. A European couple wanted to see Lake Michigan. They let Kanti keep the meter running as they ventured onto the sand. Then they decided to stay for the sunset. It was a dream fare.

Kanti explained how the European couple set up their belongings underneath an umbrella as close as possible to the water without touching it. They unloaded brightly colored towels, snacks, and many layers of clothes. They shed almost all their clothing before turning to each other. They kissed and huddled close together as they stared off into the setting sun.

"You could see everything," Kanti said. "I still dream about her."

"Did you see her front?" Hans said.

"I could see everything."

"I think we need muscles to get a girl like that," Hans said.

Kanti took a sip of beer before handing it to Hans. "The only muscle you need is here," he said, pointing to his crotch.

Sitting in the taxi aggravated Hans's back. The pain was combined with a general fatigue and dreariness that matched the gray sky. He wasn't sure if the moody weather influenced his physical ailments or if his discomfort projected the conditions outside. Studying real estate was painful. It hurt to read. Beer usually helped. He took a sip from Kanti's can.

"How far are we from the lake?" Hans said.

"Are you in a hurry?"

"I need to study."

Kanti grabbed the beer and tilted it above his head to salvage the last drop. He threw the can out the car window. "I won't let you quit your taxi shift."

"We can't keep doing this forever," Hans said. "My back already hurts."

"This taxi needs you."

"Why aren't we working today then?"

"Because you need a girl to help you relax."

"I'd rather work."

"You'll change your mind once you see the girls at the lake."

Hans followed Kanti out of habit that had developed over time. Their routine was comforting. They spoke freely in their native tongue and shared a collective memory of an abandoned home. They discovered new hobbies together, drank beer, smoked cigarettes, and listened to American music. The familiarity of a forsaken home bound their friendship.

They pulled into a nearly empty parking lot. The sun failed to break through the morning fog, as was customary for September mornings in Michigan. Hans had never seen so much water before. Back home, water was just another agricultural input, like fertilizer and pesticide. It was used for cooking, cleaning, and bathing. It simply supported survival and didn't offer the majesty of the lake. The waves crashed into the sand every few moments. The water receded faster than it arrived. The rhythm and repetition of the waves was beautiful.

Kanti removed everything from the trunk. A canister of motor oil leaked onto the asphalt. A broken umbrella was stacked on two piles of rope. Kanti handed Hans the white sheet that covered the bottom of the trunk. One side of the sheet was stained black in the shape of the tire.

"Are you ready to get some girls?" Kanti said.

"It's not that easy," Hans said.

"You never listen to me. You wouldn't have so many problems if you would just listen to me."

"I don't have any problems."

"The first step is believing we can get girls."

"What's the second step?"

"Stop studying."

Hans wondered if Kanti was the real problem. Kanti forced him to take the easy way out—to quit school, drive his taxi, and now keep him company on a pointless vacation day. Kanti constantly pulled Hans in directions he didn't want to go, but reluctantly followed anyway, with the hope they might lead somewhere better.

"I'm trying to do something nice for you and all you do is complain," Kanti said.

"I never asked you to bring me here."

Kanti lodged his foot in the sand with a few aggressive kicks. "This will do," he said, handing Hans one end of the stained white sheet. They spread the sheet on the sand and used their shoes to anchor the corners.

Hans's knees cracked as he stumbled to a cross-legged position on the sheet. He pulled the real estate book from his pocket and started reading.

"You're wasting your time," Kanti said. "We're taxi drivers."

It wasn't worth explaining anything to Kanti. He never listened. Hans was determined to show Kanti that he was more than just a taxi driver.

"Here come the girls," Kanti said. "Let me do the talking."

"My English is better than yours," Hans said.

"Trust me."

Two girls swayed between the sand and water with ease. The tall one was blonde like a Hollywood model and wore a two-piece floral swimsuit. Hans couldn't see everything like Kanti promised, but almost everything, just like the girls in the magazines. The short one tied her wavy brown hair tightly in a bun. Her faded denim shorts covered her one-piece swimsuit.

"I'll take the tall one," Kanti said. He stood up and tightened his T-shirt sleeves until the cloth covered his hairy armpits. Hans undid the top two buttons of his shirt to reveal a few curly chest hairs.

"Hello, ladies," Kanti said.

The girls stopped in front of their white sheet.

"Good day to party at the beach," Hans said.

The tall girl covered her mouth with both hands, glanced at her friend, and laughed. Her cheeks dimpled. She was perfect. Hans despised Kanti for claiming the tall one. Kanti always left Hans with nothing worth having. Lately it had been the taxi shifts on holiday weekends and now the most beautiful blonde girl Hans had ever seen.

"You look too young to party," the short girl said.

"Is it our accents? Are they funny?" Hans said.

The short girl touched Hans's elbow. "Your accents are adorable."

"Where are you from?" the tall girl said.

"Close by," Kanti said. "Inland, on the Michigan side."

"Does everyone on the Michigan side have your accent?"

"We're from India," Hans said. "The north part."

Hans recognized Kanti's glare from high school. It meant stop talking. Hans ignored him. Things were going well for him with the tall girl.

"Do you want to swim with us?" the short girl said.

"He can't swim," Kanti said.

The tall girl reached for her friend's hand. "We're getting in the water," she said.

The short girl's swimsuit was backless. She untied her bun to cover the freckles on her neck, took off her shorts, and jogged toward the water. Both girls briefly disappeared after diving headfirst into the lake.

"I told you to let me do the talking," Kanti said.

"Why did you tell them I can't swim?" Hans said.

"Why did you tell them about India?"

"You're always getting in the way."

"I'm showing you how it's done."

Hans sat down on the sheet. "How long are we staying here?"

"Relax. The girls will come back if we ignore them."

"Then what will happen?"

"Everything will happen if you follow me."

Hans flipped the pages of his book. It was impossible to focus over the thunderous waves of the lake. "Did we bring any water?"

"Girls are everywhere," Kanti said. "Look at that one over there."

Hans squinted against the glistening clouds. There were several families, a couple dogs, and girls of all ages. Most people lounged in the sand, but a few were in the water. The lake formed a devouring glow behind the people standing by the water. The clouds perched as low as the tide, forming a gray wall between the shore and whatever lay beyond.

"I'm getting some water," Hans said.

"You'll drown," Kanti said.

Hans felt himself sinking in the sand with every step until the cold waves smothered his feet. He marched into the lake until the water was up to his waist. He closed his eyes, bent his knees, and squatted until the surface of the water met his lips.

"Let the lake relax you," Kanti said from their white sheet.

Hans parted his lips and sucked the water into his mouth until it filled his cheeks. He held the water until it became warm. He swallowed. He repeated this maneuver until the lake water quenched his thirst.

The tall girl walked toward him. The water came up to her thighs. Her entire body was wet. Hans wanted to touch her everywhere.

"I thought you couldn't swim," she said.

"I should learn," Hans said.

"With all your clothes on?"

"Sorry," Hans said as he fumbled with the buttons of his shirt. He felt uncoordinated and unstable, like he could fall at any moment. He focused on the tall girl, wanting to rest his head on her bare shoulder, stand on his toes, and whisper the names of all the real estate investments he would make in her name. They could walk to the beach holding hands and he would draw out the mansions, business parks, and apartment complexes he would buy and sell for her. After today, his success would also be her victory.

"Let me help you," she said. She stepped closer and lifted Hans's hands away from the buttons. She unbuttoned his shirt and tied it around her waist like a towel. He liked how it looked on her, like she was an extension of him.

"Now, lay here," she said, extending both arms above the water.

"I'm fine standing up," Hans said.

"You don't trust me?" she said.

"I like you."

The tall girl blushed. "On my arms."

Blushing was a good sign. Hans had seen it in Hollywood movies. He was happy to steal the tall girl from Kanti. He leaned over and rested his chest on her forearms. Her other arm slid to Hans's waist. "You're wearing pants," she said, laughing.

Hans hesitated to lift his feet up.

"Jump up," the tall girl said.

Hans relied on her reassuring tone. He sensed her comfort in the water. She reminded him of the taxi customers that practiced speaking English with him—patient, calm, and nurturing. Hans lifted one of his legs. She angled her arm under his thighs to lift him up. Her forearm clenched underneath him. She was stronger than Hans imagined.

"I'm a lifeguard," she said. "This is how I teach kids to swim."

"How old are you?" Hans said.

She laughed again. "Didn't anyone teach you to never ask a girl that question?"

Hans straightened his legs and stretched his arms in the water as he lay flat on her arms. He was weightless in the water. The pressure of his real estate studies momentarily disappeared in the tall girl's arms.

"Am I swimming?" Hans said.

"Try kicking your feet," she said.

The water splashed violently when Hans kicked. Swimming was relaxing.

"Keep your feet underwater," the tall girl said, as she lifted Hans closer to the surface of the water. "It's easier if you put your face in the water."

"I can't do that," Hans said.

"I won't let you drown."

Hans believed her.

"Flip over," she said. "Let's try again."

He raised his belly to the surface as instructed and flapped his arms sideways to avoid sinking. The cool water soothed the cramping in his lower back. Sitting all day in the cab took its toll on his body. The taxi work was aging him, which was another reason to switch to real estate. He wondered if the lake was for sale. He wanted to buy it for the tall girl. They could take turns holding each other in the water, forgetting about their struggles on land.

"I'm going to let go," she said.

"I'll die," Hans said.
"Don't panic."
"I'm relaxed."
"Trust me."

Hans felt her hand leave his hairy back. He raised his chin and continued looking up at the infinite sky before his midsection caved in the water. The tall girl grabbed his hands as they swung wildly in the air. The water overwhelmed his nostrils and eyes. Gravity was compromised. Up was down. Left was right. Comfort became chaos until the girl pulled him against her soft naked flesh. Hans wrapped his arms around her neck and held onto her with his eyes closed.

"It's just water," she said, laughing again.

"I told you not to let go," Hans said, breathing heavily while regaining his footing on the sand.

She angled him toward the beach. They walked side by side, in each other's arms. "Let me take you to a safer place," she said.

Hans followed her. She untied his shirt from her waist and put it on. It fell off her shoulders and covered her sandy thighs. The sand inclined and formed a massive hill as they walked away from the water. The hill's shadow lingered over the lake. She gracefully conquered the incline while Hans slid backward after each step and dropped on all fours as he approached the top.

"What is this place?" Hans said.

"It's a dune," she said. "It's my favorite place."

The distant horizon made the beach look small. Kanti was no longer on the white sheet. He was probably chasing other girls, trying to force himself on them rather than listening and letting them make the first move. Kanti's advice never paid off. Hans was better off on his own. He noticed his real estate book in the pile of stuff on the sheet. It would have been pleasant to read it on the dune, with its view of possibilities.

The tall girl shoveled dirt from the base of a thin tree to reveal two cans of beer. She dusted the cans off on his shirt and handed one to Hans.

"To your first swimming lesson," she said.

"You come here often?" Hans said.

"It's my second home during the summer."

Hans liked how her cheeks dimpled when she clenched her lips around the beer can. "I like looking at you," he said.

She laughed. "You really need to get better at this."

"You don't mind that I look at you?"

"Why would I mind?"

"People usually don't like it when a guy like me looks at a girl like you."

"It's a free country," she said. "You can look wherever you want."

They sat on the sand, facing the lake. Only the sound of slurping warm beer interrupted the pounding waves below. The girl swayed closer to Hans as her can emptied. His back pain dissipated after each sip.

"I love India," she said.

"What do you like about it?" Hans said.

"Your dark eyes, mocha skin, strong bone structure, bushy eyebrows. It's all so great."

Hans understood that his features were unique in Michigan, but he never considered them worthy of praise. There were millions like him back home. For the first time, his appearance was appreciated. He had learned that you always returned compliments in America. "I like your body," he said.

She smiled, took Hans's hand, and forced it against her thigh. "Am I the first girl you've been with?" she said.

"Now you're asking the wrong questions," Hans said.

"First white girl then?"

"Am I your first Indian?"

"There's nobody else like you around here."

Hans grazed her leg with the back of his hand as she rested her head on his shoulder. His muscles tightened as he tried to steady her. She had taught him to swim and brought him to her favorite place. It was finally happening for him. This was America. A beer in hand. A lake. A beautiful tall girl.

Suddenly, Hans sensed red and blue flashing lights on his back. A siren beeped twice. The police officer's boots squished on the sand. Her khaki cowboy hat matched her button-up shirt and brown pants. The badge on her shirt displayed her name. Officer Kelly Miller.

"What are you doing out here?" Officer Kelly said.

Hans and the girl faced Officer Kelly.

Officer Kelly shined a flashlight at them. "Where's your shirt?" she said.

Hans looked down at his chest. He remembered the tall girl's soft touch when she unbuttoned his shirt. She was still wearing the shirt like it was her own.

"Have you been drinking this evening?"

Hans dropped the can and turned to the girl, hoping she would say something to defend them. "No, ma'am," he said.

"Sarah, get in the car," Officer Kelly said. "I'm taking you home to your parents."

The girl left Hans's side and walked toward the officer.

"You know her?" Hans said.

"Don't talk to her," Officer Kelly said. "Don't even look at her."

"Please, Aunty," Sarah said.

"Aunty? Are you related?"

"You're under arrest as soon as I send her home."

Arrest? A criminal record could end Hans's realty dream. Nobody would trust a criminal with the buying or selling of their property. Hans tried thinking about his crime but couldn't recall any grave mistakes. He'd given up valuable study time to relax at the beach with his friend.

Sarah had given him a swimming lesson. What crime had he committed?

Officer Kelly spoke directly to Sarah. "Did he hurt you?"

"Let me explain," Sarah said.

"Your parents are going to be very disappointed," Officer Kelly said.

"How does this officer know your parents?" Hans said.

"Shut up," Officer Kelly said. "Did he force you to drink?"

Sarah wrapped her arms around her waist so tightly that Hans's shirt covered her midriff. For the first time that day, Hans couldn't stare at her chest. "Yes," she said.

"That's a lie," Hans said.

"I don't know where you're from, but I decide what's the truth in this town," Officer Kelly said.

"She gave me the beer."

"Sarah, honey, look at me. Don't look at him. I'm in charge here. Look at me."

"I don't know where the beer came from," Sarah said.

"What else did he do to you?"

"Nothing," Hans said. "I don't even know where to touch her."

"Go home, Sarah," Officer Kelly said. "And we'll never speak of this again."

Sarah obeyed her aunt. The confidence she'd showcased in the water had vanished. She sagged her shoulders, bowed her head, and disappeared behind the police car. Officer Kelly whispered something into the radio on her chest.

Hans felt betrayed. Sarah had taken advantage of him. Where was Kanti? He would know how to get out of this situation. Kanti wasn't good for much, but he was good at lying to Americans.

"I didn't say you could go," Officer Kelly said.

"I'm getting my book from the beach and going home."

Officer Kelly pointed her gun at Hans. "You have the right to remain silent," she said. "Anything you say can and will be used against you."

Hans raised his hands and shuffled his feet toward the dune. "This is a misunderstanding."

"This is your final warning."

Hans tripped over his own feet, regained his balance, and darted down the dune. Officer Kelly tackled him from behind, causing him to roll down the hill. He tasted blood in his mouth as he fell onto the sand and lost consciousness.

Hans was awake but couldn't open his left eye. The swelling started in his gums and extended up his cheekbone into the eye socket. He rested his head against the water-stained wall. A tube light flickered above him. His vision was blurry. The people on the other side of the steel bars were dressed in identical khaki outlines. Hans wore the same shirt as the officers. His shirt said "Volunteer" on the breast pocket.

Officer Kelly approached the cell door. "Let's call it even," she said. "You weren't forcing my niece to drink at the beach, and I didn't tackle you."

"I didn't do anything wrong."

"Neither did I."

Hans considered her offer and his lost future with Sarah. This was the best deal for his real estate career. "Can I go home now?"

"We called you a cab," Officer Kelly said.

Hans followed Officer Kelly to the steel door at the side of the building. She held it open for him.

"Did you get my book?" Hans said.

Officer Kelly nudged her head toward the cold air outside. "The shirt is a gift," she said. "Stay out of trouble."

Hans recognized the roar of the engine outside. The taxi sign was back on top of the car.

"What took you so long?" Kanti said. He looked in the rearview mirror at Officer Kelly. "She's got a body. Did you get her number?"

"Just shut up for once," Hans said.

The gate opened in front of them. Kanti saluted the attendant and exited the parking lot. "Don't you want to know what happened after you left?"

Hans shifted in his seat until the warm air from the vent blew directly into his face.

"The tall girl came back," Kanti said.

Hans closed his eyes.

"She showed me this path at the foot of the dune," Kanti continued. "A real narrow wooded path. You'd miss it if you didn't know it was there."

Kanti was lying again. Pathetic.

"We kept walking down the path. I'm getting nervous now. Where is she taking me? Is she going to kill me? She could have if she wanted to. She was so tall."

Hans wished she had killed him.

"Then she grabbed my hand and pulled me into this bush. But it wasn't a bush at all. It was another path that went deeper into the trees. There's no way I could find it again."

Hans began to recognize the streets surrounding his apartment complex. He noticed "For Sale" signs on a few vacant lots. He tried memorizing the phone numbers on the signs but Kanti's lies competed for his attention.

"We laid down on this small patch of sand. It was perfect sand. Soft and fluffy, like a mattress."

Hans wasn't sure if he wanted to practice residential or commercial real estate. There was big money in commercial, but the inventory in residential was higher.

"Then everything happened. Sideways. Backwards. Forwards. You imagine it, and we did it," Kanti said. "I know you liked the tall girl too. But I called her first."

The white sheet was crumpled in the backseat, but Hans didn't see his book.

"You know, I'm on duty right now," Kanti said.

The accelerated uptick of the meter made Hans dizzy. Kanti's riders were at the mercy of the cheating red numbers. There was no way the meter went this fast during Hans's rides. Kanti must have sped it up. He was lying to his customers too.

"The short girl was asking about you," Kanti said.

Hans rolled down his window.

"You could've had fun with her if you'd listened to me."

Kanti pulled into Hans's apartment complex.

"Where's my book?" Hans said. "It was on the white sheet."

"I told you to forget that nonsense," Kanti said.

Hans opened the glove compartment. Inside, there was an empty pack of cigarettes, a gun, and a book with a naked man and woman entangled together on the cover.

"A nice girl would help you relax," Kanti said. "I heard we need to join a gym to find the really nice girls."

Hans got out of the cab.

Kanti stopped the meter. "How about we call it even on the window?" he said, pointing to Hans's bedroom. "This ride back home for the window. How about it?"

Hans stood outside the cab. He needed to find a new real estate book. He could only rely on his studies. Nobody else could help him now. He slammed the cab door. The harsh metallic sound vibrated between buildings and echoed into the night sky, escaping to the shores of the lake, where it would easily be absorbed by the crashing waves. Hans once again promised himself that tomorrow he'd start working on his dreams.

DINNER PARTY

Hans and Neelam arrived late to her parents' lake house. The silence and stillness of the neighborhood bothered Hans. It was eerie compared to the lively overflow of immigrants and shift laborers that trafficked his apartment complex in the city, hours east of Lake Michigan.

A few houses had colored Christmas lights lining the gutters above their garages. All the houses had a few inches of snow piled up against their entrances. Fireplaces flickered behind pale curtains and windows angled toward the frozen lake. Hans cautiously held the dashboard with both hands as Neelam drove to her house along the narrowly shoveled part of the driveway. The garage opened from the inside as she turned off her car.

"Are you ready?" Neelam said.

"What if I failed the exam?" Hans said.

Neelam pinched Hans's cheeks. "Can you forget the exam for a few hours tonight? This is important to me."

"What do I need to do?"

"Behave and don't drink too much," she said.

"Anything else?"

"Eat whatever you're given and wear what you're gifted."

"That's a lot."

"Hans, please."

"I'm not good with your friends."

"This is my family," Neelam said.

"That's worse."

"Follow my lead. Let's go."

Neelam's mother stood by the door in a black dress that came down to her knees. Her gray cardigan was slightly darker than her white pearl earrings and matching necklace. Her lips were shiny, even without lipstick. "You're late," she said, leaning to hug Neelam without stepping onto the cold concrete of the garage. "Your father is upset."

"The roads are really bad downstate," Neelam said.

Hans was surprised by Neelam's response. The roads were clean, and the snow had stopped in the morning. Neelam had driven over the speed limit. They arrived as fast as they could. Hans followed her lead. "It's that time of the year," he said.

"And you must be Hans." Neelam's mother leaned forward and pushed her cheeks against his. "We're so happy you're spending the holidays with us."

Hans felt her warmth emanating from her smile and the delicacy of her voice. He now better understood the origin of Neelam's kindness.

Neelam's mother gently kissed Hans on his forehead as she held his shoulders. "So handsome. I'm Dal."

"Is that your full name?" Hans said.

"It was Daljeet in our country but it's been Dal since we got here."

"Let us in," Neelam said. "It's cold."

The garage door closed behind Hans as he walked into the house. It was warm inside. They were led to the kitchen through the laundry room. The dinner table was set with a green tablecloth and four red napkins. It was lit with Christmas themed candles. Santa Claus, Frosty, reindeer, and a few elves were huddled together inside a large wreath in the center of the table. Hans thought these Christmas scenes were reserved for American movies, not real life.

"Where's Dad?" Neelam asked.

"He went to his study when you didn't arrive on time," Dal said. "You know how he is."

"Dad's always upset about something."

"Will you show Hans to his room? Don't take too long up there. Dinner's almost ready."

Each wooden step squeaked as Hans and Neelam carried their bags upstairs. They were greeted by family photos at the top of the stairwell. The family had attended many football games together and once visited the Eiffel Tower. Neelam had a gap between her two front teeth for most of her childhood. She had been Barbie for Halloween at least twice. Dal looked the same in all the pictures. Her smile appeared colorful even in the black-and-white images.

Neelam's dad had lost his hair at a young age and often posed with his boat, *Lady Liberty*. There was no indication that the family came from a foreign land. If Hans didn't know any better, he would've assumed their brown skin was just a tan from summers spent on the lake.

"This is a very nice house," Hans said. "Are you rich?"

"Stop it," Neelam said.

"Your mom thinks I'm handsome."

"So do I," Neelam said, as she reached behind to tickle Hans's belly.

Hans suddenly felt a cold hand squeezing his shoulder. The grip loosened when he turned around. Unlike the clean-shaven pictures, Neelam's dad now had a politely trimmed beard. "You're late," he said.

"I'm sorry, sir," Hans said.

"Dad. What's on your face?" Neelam placed her palms on his cheeks. "You're so hairy," she said. Neelam threw herself into her dad's arms. He rubbed his cheeks up and down Neelam's face until she shrieked.

"Stop. It scratches."

Neelam's dad was taller than Hans. His muscular chest burst out of his red turtleneck sweater. Hans had driven men like him many times in his taxi. They had pristine haircuts, wore dry-cleaned clothes, were always in a hurry, and possessed an air of arrogance that derived from self-importance. Hans imagined that he was a great tipper.

Neelam's dad shook Hans's hand forcefully. Hans felt the futility of his own grip.

"Tardiness is a weakness," he said. "I'm Pam."

"There's so much construction on the roads right now," Neelam said.

"Is Pam short for something?" Hans said.

"It's just Pam."

"Dad, we just got here. Let me show Hans to his room."

"I'll be downstairs pouring us some wine. You like wine, don't you?" Pam said.

"I love wine," Hans said.

"We'll have a glass or two," Neelam said.

"Come on, it's the holidays," Pam said.

Neelam grabbed Hans's hand and pulled him toward a room at the end of the hallway.

There was a bookshelf facing the entrance to the bedroom. The top shelves contained travel books. London, Paris, Rome—all the major cities. The bottom shelves were filled with framed photos of *Lady Liberty* over the years. A single bed was centered in the room between two end tables. The lamp on one of the end tables was shaped like an anchor.

"Your family travels a lot," Hans said, as he skimmed the spines on the bookshelf.

"Don't drink too much," Neelam said.

"I have to keep your dad company."

"You don't have to keep up with him."

"I finished my exam. I need to relax."

"It's important to me that they like you."

"They will like me more after a drink or two."

"Hans, stop it. I know how you can get."

"Would you like me if I had a beard?" Hans said.

"I've never seen you with a beard."
"What if I had one like your Dad's?"
"My Dad looks like a goof. You're handsome."

Neelam stepped on his feet to meet him nose to nose. She gently grazed Hans's face with the back of her fingers. She kissed his cheeks. Her lips were dry and chapped from the cold. He felt warm and grounded in her presence.

Neelam was the best thing that had ever happened to Hans. She had encouraged him to study to become a realtor during his taxi shifts. When Hans struggled with the math, she guided him through it. She often stayed over late and quizzed him on realty concepts. Zoning, commercial versus residential, floor plans, square footage—she never let him sleep until he had rehearsed them all. She wrote important equations on colored Post-it notes and displayed them all over the walls of his otherwise bland apartment. She inhabited his dreams, but this was the first time he had entered her world. Her world was different. It was orderly, clean, and beautiful—just like her. Everything was exactly where it needed to be. The house made sense because she came from it.

"I like you as you are and my parents will too," Neelam said.

"Even with a beard?"

"No beard. Now get changed for dinner."

Hans dumped the contents of his bag on the single bed, scattering an assortment of receipts and study notes across the floral covers. His camera landed on the pillow. He put the lighter and pack of cigarettes in his pocket and stretched a thick yellow sweater across the bed. Neelam had bought him the sweater the previous weekend and insisted that he wear it at dinner. He opened both drawers of the end table. They were empty. Hans dropped to his knees and lifted the bed skirt. There was nothing underneath the bed. He wasn't accustomed to the emptiness of the room. There was more clutter in his own life. It had been worse before Neelam. He still resorted to his old habits of drinking and smoking on the rare days that she didn't visit. But he strived to be better for her.

Hans cautiously approached the walk-in closet. A light automatically switched on when he entered. Most of the hanging clothes were wrapped in plastic dry-cleaning bags. He flipped through them and stopped at a red sari. Many of the plastic sparkles were intact on the short blouse. The blouse wasn't long enough to cover the stomach. The waistline of the skirt was petite. The matching chunni was patterned and heavier than Hans's winter coat. He wondered how Neelam would look in the sari. He'd never seen her in Indian clothes. She usually wore jeans with a T-shirt or tank top. Her simplicity was endearing.

There was a knock on the door.

"Are you ready to come down?" Neelam said.

Hans pulled the plastic cover over the sari. "I need more time," he said.

"Hurry up. I'll be downstairs."

Hans heard Neelam skip down the stairs. He closed the closet door and retrieved his cigarettes. He opened the window at the foot of the bed and lit one. Outside, the air was brisk and still. The tree branches were covered in a soft powdery snow. The lake appeared frozen around the edges of the docks leading back to each house.

Hans carefully blew smoke out the window. The smoke aligned with the warm fumes from the furnace below. He hastened the length of his puffs to expedite a head buzz. Like with coffee and alcohol, the faster the better. The cigarette awakened his appetite for wine.

Hans closed the window and breathed into his palms. His breath smelled like cigarette smoke. He rummaged through his belongings until he found his Chanel cologne. It was the first gift Neelam had given him after they started dating.

Hans opened the lid and sprayed the cologne across the yellow sweater in small bursts, concentrating the splashes around the neck and armpits. He wiped the rim of the bottle with his index finger. He brought his wet finger to his lips and rubbed the cologne on his teeth. The cologne burned his mouth. The burning was refreshing. Hans licked the rim of the bottle and swirled the drops in his mouth. The sweater and his breath both smelled better.

Hans heard Neelam's laughter as he walked downstairs.

"We thought you had fallen asleep up there," Pam said.

"Not at all, sir. I was changing."

"What a beautiful sweater," Dal said, from the kitchen.

Neelam sat at the dinner table with Pam. Her teeth were already stained with wine.

Hans walked straight to the kitchen to help Dal, just as Neelam had instructed him on their drive. The dark marble counters matched the lime green tiled backsplash around the kitchen. A row of cookbooks sat on a shelf beneath an assortment of pots and pans hanging from the ceiling. Neelam's elementary school drawings were displayed on the stainless-steel fridge.

Hans barely remembered doing work at school in India. He did math on a personal chalkboard one problem at a time. They had one notebook for language arts that had to stay with the teacher, who also served as the village post officer. There was never anything material to bring home.

"Is there anything I can help with?" Hans said.

"My dear, not in this house," Dal said. "You can help by joining Neelam and Pam in the dining room."

Hans remained in the kitchen. He made eye contact with Neelam in the next room. She approved of his willingness to help.

"If you insist, you can grate this cheese." Dal passed him a plate with a grater and block of cheese.

"I would love to," Hans said.

Neelam laughed loudly in the dining room. Pam clapped every time she laughed. Hans couldn't hear what they were saying.

"Are they always like this together?" Hans said.

"They get louder as the night goes on," Dal said. She put another block of cheese on his plate. "How did you meet my daughter?"

Hans wasn't sure what Neelam had told her parents.

"Didn't she tell you?"

"She's very private with her relationships."

"Have there been others?"

"I guess she's private with you too," Dal said. "Don't worry. You're the first Indian."

Hans had never asked Neelam about her previous relationships. She never mentioned other boys.

"She met the last one at a bar on karaoke night. They connected over a Bob Seger song," Dal said. "How did you two meet?"

Pam and Neelam ran into the kitchen before Hans could answer. They each held a bottle of wine.

"Red or white, Hans?" Pam said.

"Give him red, Dad. A little bit."

Hans took the glass from Pam and immediately took a gulp. The wine exaggerated the burning in his mouth.

Neelam sloppily scooped a handful of shredded cheese into her mouth. She massaged Hans's shoulders and whispered "thank you" in his ear.

"Dad, get over here. Bring your glass. Mom, you too," Neelam said.

The three of them gathered around Hans as he grated the cheese at the counter. "Lift your glass, young man," Pam said.

Hans put down the block of cheese and lifted his glass.

"To your first visit to our home," Pam said. "May you learn to be on time."

"Get over it, Dad," Neelam said. "I told you there was an accident on the road."

The three of them closed their eyes as the glasses approached their lips. Hans took a sip with his eyes open. His gestures were deliberate. He always wanted to do the right thing to make Neelam happy.

"Cheers," they all said.

Dal sprinkled the shredded cheese on the pasta and they all headed to the dining room. The cheese melted by the time it was Hans's turn to serve himself. There were bowls of potatoes, steamed vegetables, and a thick soup with indistinct chunks of meat. Hans couldn't remember the last time he'd had such a feast. He was accustomed to smaller meals that he finished in his taxi while driving home to his one-bedroom apartment. This food had a shine and glow that awakened his appetite. Hans decided it was okay to eat meat on this one occasion, despite the astrologer's warning.

"A glass of wine with dinner?" Pam said.

"Dad, don't do this."

"It's up to him."

"Of course," Hans said. "This tastes like expensive wine."

"Last one," Neelam said.

During dinner, Hans answered questions about his background and upbringing in India. Pam and Dal said they could relate to his history. They were familiar with the streets, smells, and lack of opportunity. Hans felt close to them based on complexion and history but not in their mannerisms. Their familiarity felt foreign. Pam and Dal had not been back home in over three decades. They had lived by the lake for too long.

"I have everything I need here," Pam said. "I have nothing to go back for."

"Don't you miss it, sir?"

"Miss what? The overpopulation? The smell of sewage?"

"I miss the food," Hans said.

"Do you not like what we served tonight?" Dal said. "I can make you something else."

"That's not what I meant. This has all been great," Hans said.

"Look at this house," Pam said. "Look out the window at the lake. You can't live like this in India." He reached across the table and held Neelam's hand. "Neelam was born here. She's always going to be here. We want to stay close to her," he said.

"What about the people?" Hans said. "Your friends and family?"

"You know how they are," Pam said.

"What do you mean?" Neelam said. "How are they?"

"Let me tell you something about Indian people," Pam said. "Indian people are corrupt. They took the world's greatest democracy and smothered it with their selfishness. That's why we have so much corruption and no progress. It's in the people's dirty natures."

"Things are getting better back home," Hans said.

"Then why are you here?" Pam said. "Why did you leave your friends and family for the snow?"

"Just because he's here, doesn't mean he can't miss home," Dal said. "I still miss things about India."

"Since when?" Pam asked. "What do you miss?"

"I miss my family."

"What family?" Neelam said. "I didn't know we had family in India."

Pam stood up and poured everyone another glass of wine. "They aren't real family," he said. "Distant uncles and cousins. They are nobodies."

"They might not mean anything to you, but I grew up with them. They are my family," Dal said.

"Why haven't they ever visited us?" Neelam said.

"Why don't you ask your father why we've never gone back?" Dal said.

"Mom is right. You never took us to India."

Pam shook his head and took another sip of wine. "Nobody has done less with more than India," he said. "There's nothing there for you."

Dal reached for Pam's hand. He pulled it back to his lap before she could grab it. "Do you plan on going home to India after your studies?" Dal asked.

"I finished my studies today," Hans said.

"That's wonderful!" Pam said. "What did you study? Engineering? Medicine? Law?"

"Real estate," Neelam said. She proudly turned to Hans and caressed his hand.

"What type of real estate will you practice?" Pam said.

Hans was considering residential or commercial real estate. Residential would be more profitable in a luxury lakeside neighborhood like this one. "I'm not sure yet," he said. "I've been thinking about this dune on the west side of the state, right on the lake. There's value there."

"That's public land. You can't sell government property," Pam said.

"He knows that, Dad. It was an idea."

"Have you considered government infringement on private property? The government is taking our land. Private property rights are being abolished," Pam said.

Hans looked at Neelam. He wanted her to answer. "No politics after six p.m., Dad. You know the rules."

"It's not politics. It's an inevitability. We need to be ready for it."

"Nobody answer him," Neelam said.

Hans looked up to see Pam staring at him, demanding an answer. Hans ignored his gaze and served himself more potatoes.

Pam took another sip of wine. "This is probably a good time to tell you. Your mom and I are thinking about selling the house," he said.

"What?" Neelam said, pouring herself another glass of wine. "You can't do that. I grew up in this house."

"You don't come home much, and the house is too big for the two of us," Dal said. "Plus, we could be closer to you in the city."

Hans started seeing the house differently. Home buyers loved being near water. He could sell this place in a day, maybe over the asking price if Pam and Dal were patient. If Hans passed his realty exam, this would be the first place he'd put on the market.

"I love this house," Neelam said. "Dad, tell me you're lying."

"The neighbors said we can still use the lake. We will keep our boat."

Hans thought the linoleum in the kitchen needed to be replaced with hardwood before listing the house. More color in the kitchen could help too.

"I don't care about your stupid boat," Neelam said. "We can't sell this house."

"You can get great value for it if you sell now," Hans said. "It's a seller's market."

Neelam slapped Hans on the shoulder. "Whose side are you on?" she said.

"Nothing is official," Pam said. "We can talk about this later."

"We'd rather hear more about you two," Dal said. "How long have you been together now?"

"About four months," Hans said.

Neelam nodded. "It's been amazing."

"How did you meet?" Pam asked.

This time Neelam spoke quickly. She was prepared for the question. "You know how I've always loved photography?" She squeezed Hans's knee under the table. "One day on campus, I saw a stranger taking pictures of the trees. He was so careful and gentle with his approach. I went over and talked to him and here we are."

"How long have you been doing photography?" Pam asked.

"It's just a hobby. It's an old camera. I bought it used," Hans said.

"We're going to start learning photography together," Neelam said.

It was true that Hans had purchased a used camera, but the rest of the story was a lie. Hans and Neelam had met at Tables, a local bar around the corner from his apartment. It was a Tuesday. Hans sat alone at a table staring up at the lottery numbers on the blurry television. Neelam walked in with two other girls. The bar was empty, but they still asked to join Hans. The girls wore thick wool coats with silk scarves and high heels. They were dressed much nicer than the typical customers at Tables. Hans became conscious of his English around them. The other girls called him "Hands." Neelam corrected them and remained curious about Hans while the other girls got bored and started playing pool. Neelam kept buying drinks so Hans kept talking. He told her about his sister Aarti, about his best friend Kanti, and how he wanted to quit driving a taxi to pursue a career in real estate. Neelam listened long after her friends had left and all the way back to the single mattress on the floor of Hans's apartment.

Hans wondered what else Neelam lied about. She acted differently around her parents and distanced herself from truth. He was losing her to the customs of the home. He felt like she was ashamed of him.

Pam brought four tiny glasses from the kitchen. He poured the contents of a colorful bottle into each of the glasses. The liquid smelled like lemon and mint.

"This is the bottle of limoncello we got in Italy last summer," Neelam said. "It's one hundred percent organic." She downed it like a shot, then immediately placed her glass in front of Pam for a refill.

Hans took a sip. It tasted like sweetened lemon cough syrup. "It's different," he said.

"It's a refined taste," Pam said. "It's acquired over time."

"It's getting late," Dal said. "Neelam, will you help me with the dishes?"

"Do I have to?"

"Help your mother," Pam said. "Earn your wine tonight."

Neelam slouched her shoulders and stomped her feet as she followed Dal into the kitchen. Pam and Hans remained at the table. Hans thought this was his opportunity to say something clever. Maybe go back to the private property topic or insist that he didn't want to go back to India either. He wanted to stay here by the lake too. Pam spoke before Hans had a chance.

"Are you going to invite me out for a cigarette?" Pam said.

"Cigarette?" Hans said.

"Oh, come on. I wasn't born yesterday. The cologne didn't work." Pam spoke louder now. His words were more intentional and cutting. The gracious host transformed into the protector of the house. "I don't believe the photography story. That's something my daughter saw in a movie."

"It's true," Hans said. "My camera is upstairs."

"I don't think you know a damn thing about real estate either," Pam said.

"I can sell this house."

"I don't want you anywhere near my home."

"Sir."

"Stop the sir bullshit." Pam poured himself another shot of limoncello.

"I like your daughter," Hans said.

"I don't know where my daughter found you."

"She's helped me a lot."

"The problem is that you're still one of them. The people back home who are secretly smoking cigarettes in other people's homes. You are here but your nature is still from there."

"I'm getting better," Hans said.

"I know my daughter. She's with you because she feels sorry for you. She's naive. She's in love with the idea of your struggle, not in love with you."

Pam poured Hans another shot. Hans immediately drank it. The second one stung less. Hans wanted to fight back but that went against Neelam's instructions.

"I know your kind. I grew up with your kind. You sell fake electronics on street corners. You were probably driving a taxi before you met my daughter," Pam said, after taking his shot.

"There's nothing wrong with driving a taxi," Hans said.

"We worked too hard to get here, away from people like you, to end up with you again," Pam said.

Hans reached over the table and took the bottle from Pam. He read the label. "Do you have anything stronger than this?"

Pam stood up and opened the wooden cabinet in the dining room. He brought out a bottle of whiskey. Hans didn't recognize the label.

"Tonight, you may drink my booze and eat my food. Tomorrow, I want you gone."

Hans poured himself a healthy amount of whiskey. He had heard enough. "How long did it take to lose your accent?" Hans said.

"I don't have an accent. I never did."

"Now it's my turn to call you a liar."

Pam stood up at the table. "You're not good enough for my daughter," he said.

Hans took two quick sips of the whiskey. It tasted like smoke. "Do you still want the cigarette?" he said.

The water turned off in the kitchen. Pam put the bottle of whiskey back in the cabinet.

Dal came back into the dining room. "We're so glad you came," she said. "We'll see you in the morning." She put her hand on Hans's head and stroked his hair before heading upstairs.

Pam turned to Hans with his red eyes. "It's been enlightening," he said.

"Sir, if you don't mind, I had one more question," Hans said. "Why did you leave India?"

"It was a number of things," Pam said. "But mostly it was to get away from the dishonesty. I left India to get away from people like you."

Hans raised his empty glass to him. "I hope we never forget where we came from," he said.

"You be sure to remind us."

Neelam walked into the dining room and kissed her dad before he headed upstairs.

Hans didn't want to look at Neelam. He couldn't trust her. This was all her fault. She had brought him here to embarrass him.

Neelam folded the unused napkins at the dinner table. The serene setting mimicked the many nights they spent together in his unfurnished apartment, only with fancy furniture and holiday themed table settings. She seemed completely unaware of the reality of her house. Her sanctuary was Hans's hell.

"How did we do?" Hans said.

"We are perfect together." She leaned closer to Hans. "What did you think of my parents?"

"Your mom is very kind."

"Do you feel loved by them?"

"I don't think your dad likes me."

"Are you kidding? He brought out the limoncello. That's an endorsement." Neelam suddenly stood up. "Let's go upstairs."

Neelam sped up the stairs. Hans followed slowly and stopped in the bathroom. He smiled in front of the bathroom mirror. He wiped his front teeth with his tongue to try to remove the wine stains. He leaned closer to the mirror and noticed a zit forming on his forehead. Wine gave him zits, which was why he preferred beer. He pulled his hair off his forehead. His hairline had crept up toward the middle of his scalp. It hurt when Hans scratched the fresh zit. He tried poking it with his fingernail. Then he pinched it between his thumb and index finger. The mixture of puss and blood made his fingers stick together. Maybe Pam was right. His nature was dirty.

Hans washed his bloody finger and thumb in the sink. The value of the property could be increased by switching to a modern cube sink that sat below a mirror. Forget it, Hans thought. This family didn't need him or his help.

The light in Hans's room was already on. Neelam was sitting on his bed.

"This is my room," Hans said.

"I thought this could be our room for a little bit."

"Where's all my stuff?"

"I packed it for you."

Hans took the camera, receipts, wallet, cigarettes, and lighter out of the bag and scattered them across the bed again. He sat beside Neelam. She looped her arm around Hans's elbow and rested her head on his shoulder. She reeked of her dad's wine.

"I'm sorry I lied about how we met," Neelam said, as she stroked the back of his hand.

"You're ashamed of me," Hans said.

"I want them to like you."

Neelam angled her head slightly and started kissing the side of Hans's unshaven neck. "Your dad hates liars."

Neelam stopped kissing him. "What did he say to you?"

"Your mom told me about your other boyfriends," Hans said.

"They were nobodies," Neelam said. "I'm with you now."

She even spoke like her father. Hans stood up and walked to the closet. He felt her stare at him from the bed. He opened the closet door and pulled out the red sari.

"My mom's wedding sari. How did you find that?"

Neelam lifted the plastic bag. Hans sat on the bed and watched her play with the beads and run her fingers along the patterned embroidery. He pulled out a cigarette and put it to his lips.

"Put it on," Hans said.

"You can't smoke in here," Neelam said.

Hans pointed at the sari and then at Neelam.

"Are you drunk?" she asked.

Hans lit his cigarette.

"When did you drink more?"

"I said, put it on," Hans said.

"Will you put out the cigarette if I do?"

Hans took an exaggerated puff.

Neelam turned around and opened the closet door.

"Not in there," Hans said. "Out here. In front of me."

Neelam circled the room to open all the windows. She tried waving out the cigarette smoke with her arms. "You always get like this when you drink," she said.

The refreshing cold breeze invigorated Hans. "Put it on," he said.

Neelam removed her pants and then her sweater. She shivered in her bra as she fumbled with the sari. "You're hurting me again," Neelam said, as she wiped tears off her cheeks.

Hans took the sari from her. He hovered close to her, intentionally breathing heavier so she could smell the smoke on his breath. He grabbed the corners of the cloth and stretched it out the length of his wingspan. He stood behind Neelam and wrapped the sari around her shoulders like a cape. He held her elbows and spun her around until the sari mummified her.

"I told you not to drink too much," Neelam said.

Hans stepped back and took one final look at her. Neelam had transformed his life and briefly made him a better person. He never would've taken the realtor exam without her. But he couldn't trust her after tonight. Her lies embarrassed him.

Her father's personal shame was masked in judgment. "Let me know if your parents decide to sell this house," Hans said. He left her standing in the room in the sari.

Hans picked the Paris travel book off the bookshelf, grabbed the bottle of smoked whiskey downstairs, and exited the house through the back door. The backyard connected to a walking path around the lake. He assessed each property along the path. He liked one specific lot on the north side of the lake. It was a small house with a big yard. At first, he hesitated to see if an alarm sounded or a dog chased him back onto the path before creeping around the house until he reached the dock.

Hans wondered what his life would look like without Neelam. He'd go back to playing Keno at the bar. Neelam would be fine. Maybe she would be upset for a day or two, but she would quickly forget him among the delicacies of her lake house. Her parents would keep her safe from threats like him.

Hans felt the cold air attacking his lungs as he walked onto the dock. He blamed the unfamiliar limoncello for the burning in his abdomen. The wooden planks creaked but felt stable under his feet. The frozen lake falsely inflated the value of the properties. Swigs of smoked whiskey provided momentary warmth. He had lost his first client and first love on the same day. The colorful pages of the travel book briefly focused his gaze. He promised to purchase a property in Paris one day.

TONY AND JIM'S

Jim died of a stroke a year after partnering with Tony on a pizzeria. Tony didn't change the name after Jim's sudden death. It was still called Tony and Jim's when Hans had started delivering pizzas there last winter.

Hans stomped through the uneven, snowy steps leading to Estella's crooked front porch. He had her weekly order of a cheese and mushroom panzerotti.

Estella opened the door after two knocks. Her thin curls barely covered her balding head. The collar of her white sweater was stained with dried pizza sauce. Her bifocal glasses hung on a lanyard around her neck. The loose skin of her cheeks flapped in the cold breeze.

"You're not Jim," she said.

"Jim's dead," Hans said, recounting the story of his passing. "Died in his sleep." He did this every week. Estella was old and forgetful. Hans suspected there was something else wrong with her as well.

"Jim and I are from the same region in Italy," Estella said.

During warmer days, when Hans had more patience to chat, he invented elaborate stories of Jim's death to test Estella's memory. Initially Jim drowned during an innocent beach day on Lake Michigan. Another time his arm got caught in the heavy machinery on the assembly line at General Motors, and once he was chopped up into tiny pieces by his business partner, Tony, and his body parts were used as toppings in the pizzeria. The degree of violence never shocked Estella.

"It's twenty dollars," Hans said.

Estella turned to retrieve her purse. She was a hunchback. Her spine protruded from the back of her neck and looked sharp enough to cut through her sickly skin and the wool of her sweater. Hans wanted to slide his hand along the elongated bone. He wondered if it could cut through his palm.

Estella handed Hans the bill. "Jim keeps raising the prices," she said.

"Gas keeps going up."

"Next time I want Jim to deliver to me."

Hans saluted Estella and followed his snowy footsteps back to the car. He'd only over-charged her ten dollars this week. She wouldn't remember, and he needed the extra money. His taxi shift during the day was unpredictable, and delivering pizzas at night was only profitable when there was a big football game. He had been saving for new windshield wipers to combat the stormy Michigan winters.

Hans didn't recognize the address of his next delivery. He looked it up before leaving the pizzeria. The house was in a cul-de-sac around the corner from Estella's. It was a first-time order that made his car smell like pineapple. New customers made Hans nervous. They weren't familiar with his reserved mannerisms. Passivity was his trick to lure a decent tip, but he feared that his Indian accent and beat-up sedan rarely left a good first impression.

A snow-covered boat occupied half the driveway of the house. The other half had been cleared to create a path to the front door. There was no doorbell. Hans knocked and removed the Hawaiian pizza out of the insulated delivery bag.

"Hans? Is that you?"

Hans was shocked to hear his name. He looked up to see Dal, short for Daljeet. She looked different from the last time he'd seen her. She now had short hair that rested at the lower tip of her ears and exaggerated the dark spots on her face. Her highlighted bangs parted across her forehead. Black eyeliner distracted from the wrinkles under her eyes. She was dressed simply in jeans and a sweatshirt. The exuberant formality and elegance that she had once exhibited was absent.

"Come inside. It's freezing," Dal said.

Hans had met Dal once before, at a family dinner when he'd been dating her daughter, Neelam. They had broken up that night. He never thought he'd see any of them again. "I have another delivery in the car," he said.

Dal grabbed the pizza and pulled him inside. Hans smelled the wine on her breath. Inside, stacks of empty moving boxes were piled in one corner. The rugs were still rolled up. A framed photo of Dal and Neelam was displayed in front of the television. The picture had been taken at the same lake house Hans had once visited. He remembered the lake and the dinner party vividly.

"The mess is temporary," Dal said. She spoke rapidly as she walked to the kitchen. Hans heard multiple cupboards open and close and water splash into the sink. She returned with two glasses of wine. One had lipstick smeared around the rim.

"When did you move here?" Hans said. He looked around nervously, searching for Dal's husband or Neelam, but the odd creaks and whistles of the house were induced by winter. There were no signs of life inside.

"We talked about moving to the city last Christmas, when you came over." Dal handed Hans a glass of wine. "Neelam tried calling you many times after that night."

"I can't drink," Hans said. "I'm late for my next delivery."

"I can't believe I found you here," Dal said. "Delivering pizza of all things."

"It's not what I was expecting."

"We looked for you everywhere after the dinner party," she said. "Why did you disappear?"

"Is your husband here?"

"Did he say something to you that night?"

Hans drank the wine in one gulp and handed the glass back to Dal. The wine warmed his hands and clouded his thoughts. "I have to finish these deliveries," he said.

"My husband hurt me too," Dal said.

Hans hurried out of the house and lunged into his front seat. Dal screamed something from her porch, but he couldn't hear her over the roar of his car. Dal had been kind to him when he'd first met her last Christmas and she was generous now. Neelam was also nice. He could've married Neelam, and they would've lived comfortably together under the guise of their matching skin color. But they were different. She was educated, while Hans had dropped out of high school. She spoke English with the precision of a professional American, while Hans fumbled through short sentences and often feigned understanding in social situations. She couldn't speak their native language, had never visited India, and was wealthy in an old Indian type of way. Old Indians were like Americans, in that they had been in America longer. They'd arrived decades before Hans and treated natural bodies of water as recreational playgrounds rather than necessary resources for cooking, laundry, and irrigation. Old Indians didn't have to clean their homes or wash their clothes by hand. They hired new Indians and purchased automated machines to perform their daily labor. The differences between Hans and Neelam had initially driven their compatibility. They'd always had something to discuss as they curiously explored each other's worlds. Their compromise was modern America. Happy hours, television game shows, and foreign wars in distant countries.

But Neelam's father had declared the difference irreconcilable. He didn't think Hans could learn the American way fast enough to appease his daughter. It was an issue of class. Old Indian versus new Indian. The new ones would never catch up. Hans hadn't fought back. He had snuck out the night of the dinner party and let Neelam go forever. Initially, he felt bad for abandoning her, but he soon accepted that their relationship would never work. They were too different, and he had yet to find a version of this country worth adapting for.

Later that night, Hans folded empty pizza boxes in the pizzeria basement between deliveries. He collapsed the flat cardboard sheets along the creases to create the hollow box. He stacked the boxes by size. Small, medium, large, and extra large. The process was mindless and therapeutic. No slippery roads, unruly customers, or potential mothers-in-law. Dal didn't appear to be settled in her new place. It was in a rough neighborhood with many abandoned houses and stray dogs. There was nowhere to boat in the city. The glamour of their family had been conceded. If Dal was in the city, then maybe Neelam was nearby too. But she wouldn't want to talk to Hans after his disappearance. Maybe Dal could reintroduce them, and they could start over. There was nothing more American than second chances.

Hans recognized Tony's approaching footsteps on the stairs.

"You're starting to spend a lot of time down here," Tony said. His apron was stained with pizza sauce and burn marks from the wood-fired oven. The moles on his neck made him look older than he was. The hair on his arms was graying faster than the mullet that stretched to the bottom of his neck.

Tony's suspicion bothered Hans. What did he think Hans was doing in the basement? There was nothing else to do down there but fold boxes and replace the filter in the furnace. It was impossible for Tony to know about his occasional beer between deliveries. Hans always hid the empties in his jacket and discarded them in the trunk of his car. He wondered if there were surveillance cameras in the basement that tracked his movements. "Almost done with all the mediums," he said. "We should be good for a week now."

"There's a lovely lady here to see you," Tony said. "Said she's one of your customers."

At first Hans thought it might be Estella searching for Jim, but it was impossible for anyone to call her lovely at her age or for her to drive anywhere.

"Did you mess up a delivery?" Tony said.

"It's been a normal night," Hans said.

"Customers first. The boxes can wait."

Hans followed Tony up the stairs. Dal stood by the register.

"I forgot to pay you," Dal said. She handed Hans a twenty-dollar bill.

"I'm on the clock," Hans said. "I can't talk right now."

"I want you to know that my husband is no longer in my life."

"There's nothing left between your daughter and me."

"Whatever happened, you didn't deserve it."

"Nothing happened."

"Nonsense," Dal said, invoking a motherly tone that surprised Hans.

"Your husband said I wasn't good enough for your daughter."

"And that was enough for you to disappear in the middle of the night?"

The pizza oven repeatedly opened and closed behind the register. The phone started ringing. Dal brought a lifetime of trouble and turmoil with her. She represented Hans's failed past and shattered future with Neelam. He wanted her to leave. "I have to get back to work," he said.

"When can I see you again?" Dal said.

"When you order another pizza."

"My daughter cried for weeks after you left her," she said. "The least you can do is give me five minutes to explain my family to you."

Tony called from the kitchen. Hans wanted to get rid of her. "I'll be at Tables after work, in a couple of hours," he said. "We can talk then."

"That's better," Dal said. "You were a nice boy. Keep being nice."

Dal's unexpected arrival had replaced the joy Hans felt at the end of each shift with anxiety. Her appearance was a surprise that he couldn't shake throughout the night. She interfered with his work and invoked the hurtful feelings of a forgotten past that he had buried deep in the burnt remains of his ashtray.

Hans finished his last delivery a few minutes after midnight. It was two large cheese pizzas for kids having a sleepover. A sleepy mother answered the door. Five kids surrounded her, took the pizza boxes from Hans, and ran down the stairs to the basement.

"Do you have any of your own?" she said.

"Unmarried," Hans said, holding up his left hand.

"Enjoy it while you can," she said. "Do you have change for a fifty?"

"I don't," Hans said, without consulting his wallet. Tips were the only way for him to increase his earnings.

"What kind of delivery guy doesn't carry spare change?"

The customers always had something to complain about. Tony said they were always right. Hans was tired of them.

"Just keep it," she said, handing him the fifty-dollar bill, a pleasant bonus for the end of the night. "Think of me when you have kids of your own."

"Can't afford kids if gas prices keep going up," Hans said.

It had started to snow again. Hans needed a new snow brush for his car. The bristles on the broom in his trunk weren't strong enough to scrape the ice from his windshield. He returned to the pizzeria to settle the receipts for the night. The math would determine what he could buy.

"Pepperonis to go," Tony said, handing Hans a small box of cold slices.

Hans accepted the box even though he didn't eat meat. He didn't have the courage to tell Tony that he was a vegetarian, fearing ridicule in a pizzeria that thrived on meat eaters.

"Who was that woman that came by today?" Tony asked.

"She's a first-time customer. Windermere Street, close to Estella," Hans said.

"Was her order okay?"

"Hawaiian."

"What did she want from you?"

"Just to talk," Hans said. "We're from the same area back home in India."

"She's cute. Too old for you, but perfect for me."

"She's married."

"Having a personal relationship with your customers is important for business," Tony said.

"My English isn't good enough for business."

"But she's not English."

"She's stuck between English and India."

"Maybe you can bring pizza to India."

Hans grabbed the box of pepperoni slices. "I'll see you tomorrow, Tony," he said.

Hans had never looked at Dal the way Tony suggested. But he was angry and nervous to see her tonight. Angry because he had worked relentlessly to forget Neelam and their potential future together. Now she threatened to return to his life through her mother. Nervous because it was rare for Hans to speak with another Indian, especially a woman. Since Neelam, he usually gauged women by their physical attributes. He only cared to know how they felt in his hands and arms. But he had to take Dal seriously. She was his elder and, in his culture, that automatically warranted his respect.

There were still a few cars outside Tables when Hans arrived. He suspected the regulars. Dal waved enthusiastically from one side of the bar as Hans entered. She lifted her jacket from the seat beside her and placed it on her own backrest. Her glass of wine was almost empty. Hans had never seen anyone order wine at Tables before. He was surprised they even had wine.

"I didn't think you were coming," Dal said.

"I had a last-minute delivery," Hans said. "A kids' sleepover party."

"Last time we met you were going to be a real estate agent."

"Last time we met you were married."

Dal took a sip of her wine and motioned to the bartender, Wendy, for another.

"You're behind," Dal said. Her bangs fell on her face. She immediately pushed them behind her ears.

Wendy brought Hans a beer and shot of cheap whiskey.

"You come here often?" Dal said.

"What happened to your husband?" Hans said.

"He left me, like you left my daughter."

Dal took off her boots underneath the counter. She spun her chair in Hans's direction. Her socks rubbed Hans's shins as she stretched her ankles.

Dal's touch stunned Hans. He took his shot of whiskey. "Why?"

"We told you over dinner that night," Dal said. "We wanted to downsize from the lake house and move to the city to be closer to Neelam."

Hans couldn't fathom the idea of downsizing. He came to America so he could finally have stuff like Nintendo and Nike shoes. He couldn't afford those luxury items yet, but he would never give them up once he had them.

"We bought that fixer-upper property where you delivered the pizza today."

"It's a nice house," Hans lied.

"We sold the lake house and moved into this place last summer."

Hans took a sip of his beer and angled his legs closer to Dal so she could rest her feet on his ankles. It was late. His morning taxi shift would start in a few hours. Then back to Tony and Jim's in the evening. Drinks between jobs helped him sleep for a few hours. The alcohol was dizzying, but the repetition was comforting.

Dal reached into her purse and applied moisturizer on her wrinkled hands, focusing on the loose webs between her fingers. "Neelam came over the day after I was served the divorce papers," she said. "She told me her Dad hadn't been happy for a long time."

"People here are so concerned with being happy," Hans said. "We never thought about happiness back home."

"Neelam said I never adjusted to life here," Dal said.

"People like us can't succeed."

"Her Dad wanted to be with someone who didn't resent life in America."

"The problem with America is that it's obsessed with America," Hans said.

"Neelam hasn't talked to me since."

"She was always chasing happiness too."

"She's one hundred percent on her Dad's side."

"I can't even get a ten percent tip because of how I speak."

"I kept the boat because screw him for turning my daughter against me."

Wendy brought them another beer and wine along with the bill. She looked at Dal. "Have I seen you before?"

"This is my first time here," Dal said. "Does he bring a lot of women here?"

"Not ones with nice tan skin like yours," Wendy said.

"We don't need any more drinks, Wendy," Hans said. "Go serve someone else."

"There was that one pretty college girl," Wendy said. "She looked a lot like you."

Dal turned to Hans. "Did you bring my daughter here?"

Neelam despised the smokiness of Tables. She also hated that Hans smoked cigarettes in his apartment. "I don't smoke," she would say. "You shouldn't either."

Hans didn't know how to respond. He felt no loyalty to Neelam or Dal. This was one drink to hear her story. Nothing more. "Maybe," he said.

Hans noticed the sudden sadness in Dal's face. Her cheeks sagged as she bit her lip. Her eyes swelled with tears. Despair illuminated the wrinkles on her forehead. "It's a nice place," she said.

"Why are you telling me all this?" Hans said.

"Because I thought you'd be on my side."

Hans was used to this assumption. The uniformity of foreignness. Everyone abroad lived the same life with identical struggles, and a single belief system colored with superstitious rituals.

"They're going to kick us out of here soon," Hans said.

Dal grabbed the bill in the shot glass in front of them. She pulled out a black trifold wallet and a glasses case from her purse. "I made you come here," she said. "Let me pay." Her reading glasses hid her tears and covered most of her face. She squinted behind the thick lenses as she pulled the receipt close to her face.

"Is it far or near?" Hans said.

"Only for reading small things like this," Dal said, holding up the tiny receipt.

Hans made out the amount. Dal had drank a lot.

Dal took off her glasses. She looked good for her age. Hans wasn't sure how old she was. He also didn't know what part of a person revealed their true age. Dal was thin, but weight could be misleading. Being the mother of an adult woman indicated maturity, and the glasses made her appear elderly and helpless. Tony wouldn't like her if he saw her blindly fumbling through her purse for loose cash to pay the bill. Why did Tony like her? Hans needed to ask him. He wanted to see Dal through Tony's predatory eyes.

"Are you tired?" Hans asked. Fatigue could be a determining factor of age.

"It's nice to be out," Dal said.

Hans noticed her wallet. There were many twenty-dollar bills left after she paid.

"You're not fit to drive," Hans said.

"I finally feel fine."

"I'm a professional driver for people and pizza. I'll drive you home."

"Do you have a cigarette?" she said.

"I didn't know you smoked."

"Only when I drink. It gets me through Michigan winters."

"I don't have one on me."

"Neelam told me you smoked."

"She never liked that I did."

"Neither did my ex-husband."

"I might have some at my place."

"Can we go to your place then?" Dal said.

Hans was shocked by her bold suggestion. She didn't care what other people at Tables thought of them. He couldn't remember the last time he'd cleaned his apartment or if he had anything left to drink. He could serve the cold pizza slices that Tony had given him. "It's messy," he said.

"You saw my place today," Dal said, smiling. "It can't be worse than that."

They drove the few blocks in silence. Hans's mind raced between the disorder of his apartment and Dal's intentions. What did she want from him? Neelam had stayed at his place many times, but that was different. She had made it her own. Her pile of pajamas had their own spot in the closet and her toothbrush was protected with a clear plastic cover that clasped tightly around the bristles. She had even decorated a wall with pictures of their excursions—a visit to a nearby state park, a soccer game on campus, and her college friend's birthday party.

Dal leaned on Hans as he unlocked his apartment door. He felt the warmth of her accelerated breaths on his shoulder and worried about the pace of her aging heart. Inside, the immediacy of the heat shocked them. He didn't pay for heat, so he left it on all day.

Dal stumbled around the apartment until she found the bathroom. She didn't close the door.

Hans heard splashing in the toilet and sink. He placed the cold pizza box in the fridge and quickly swiped the dirty kitchen counter with his hand. Dal had invaded his workplace and now his home. What could he get from her in return? He had never been with someone so old. She would have to make the first move. Where they came from, elders were the family leaders.

Dal came into the kitchen holding Hans's boxers. "These fell in the bathroom," she said. "They're dry."

"Old habits from back home," Hans said. "Saving electricity."

Hans was relieved to find a plastic bottle of whiskey and an old pack of cigarettes under the sink. He had hidden them from himself in a weak attempt to combat his vices. There was only one cigarette left. He gave the whiskey to Dal first. She studied the unfamiliar label with the same zeal with which she examined his desolate apartment. She uncapped the plastic top, took a sip, sighed heavily, and handed the bottle to Hans.

"Can you show me where my baby used to sleep?" she said.

Hans took a swig and pointed to his room. He followed Dal deeper into his apartment. She leaned slightly left on every step and her arms swung wildly in front of her, just like Neelam. Or maybe it was Neelam who walked just like Dal.

There was a pile of abandoned real estate books in one corner of Hans's room. The lone window had a rock-sized hole that was covered with duct tape. Most of his clothes were piled in front of the closet door. An empty Tony and Jim's pizza box served as an end table for loose change and receipts beside his single mattress on the floor. He was embarrassed by the sloppiness of his apartment. He needed to live better, but he didn't know how.

Dal took off her sweatshirt. She was wearing a tank top underneath. Her shoulders were paler than her hairy forearms. "Here?" she said.

Hans mistook her drunkenness for disappointment. "On the mattress," he said.

Dal crouched down and fluffed the lone pillow. She put her purse on the pizza box on the floor.

"When she was little, we had a mattress just like this in our bedroom. On nights when Neelam couldn't sleep, she would sneak into our room in the middle of the night." Dal fell back on the mattress.

Hans could see the exaggerated heaves of her chest. Tony was right. She was beautiful. "Why are you telling me all this?" he said.

"She did that all the way up to her sophomore year of high school." Dal closed her eyes. Her breathing steadied. She turned to her side and lifted her knees up to her chest. The small folds of her stomach crunched up together under her tank top. Her posture pushed her cleavage up over her green bra.

Hans noticed wrinkles on her chest. "You can't sleep here," he said. "This isn't a sleepover."

"Will you sleep with me like you slept with her?" Dal said.

Hans hesitated as he recalled ravenous nights with Neelam on his single mattress. That couldn't be what Dal meant. Was she making the first move? He changed his mind. If that was what she meant, then he wasn't the person to provide it for her. She needed someone closer to her age. Could she still have another child? When did women lose the ability to have kids? Hans felt too young to be a father. This wasn't his responsibility. This was alcohol speaking, not Dal. "I should drive you home," he said.

"Don't you miss being with my baby?" Dal said.

"Work keeps me busy."

"What if you could have her back for one night?"

"She'll never come back to me."

"You remind me of my baby when she was happiest," Dal said. "Let yourself be happy tonight."

If Hans closed his eyes, he could mistake her for Neelam. He moved the pizza box to the side. He would do this for the old lady just once. "She liked to be held when she slept," he said.

"Then hold me," Dal said.

Hans slid onto the mattress and conformed his body to her. She was warm but didn't flinch at the cold touch of his hand on her elbow. She pulled his hand around her soft stomach. The hairs on her neck extended below her hairline and down her spine. They were subtle and could only be seen up close. Only her uncontrollable hair growth hinted at her Indianness. In this position, with her entire body in his arms, it was impossible to tell her age. She could've been anyone in Hans's arms. A lover. A mother or sister. A daughter. A friend escaping from a lifetime of hurt. She liked pineapple on her pizza and preferred wine over water. She was a mother searching for her estranged daughter and an ex-wife overcoming withered years with her dominant husband. She was trying to forget the past while maintaining a promise for the future.

"Sometimes she held me too," Hans said. He lifted his neck to see Dal's expressionless face. She snored softly.

Hans stood up and paced the apartment. What if something happened to Dal tonight? Old people were always at risk for a heart attack. What would people think if she was found injured or impaled in his room? He would be accused of murder. He could get deported. He didn't like it here, but he didn't want to go back, either.

Hans stopped in the kitchen for pizza. He peeled the pepperoni off the slices and piled them in the corner of the box. He took small bites in case he missed a piece of meat under the cold cheese.

Dal's snoring intensified. Hans circled the room. He kicked his extra clothes on the floor against the wall. He sat cross-legged beside the mattress and pulled Dal's black leather purse into his lap. He unzipped it. She didn't carry a weapon. Maybe she could inflict harm with a nail file. Hans didn't recognize the assortment of makeup products in the purse. Her glasses were heavier than they looked. He felt blind with them on just as Dal probably felt blind with them off. Her trifold wallet opened as he fumbled through her belongings. He took two twenty-dollar bills. He opened the empty pizza box beside his mattress and placed the bills inside with the rest of his savings. He wasn't stealing. The money was for his ride and hospitality. A taxi and hotel room would have cost Dal the same, probably more.

Hans picked up her sweatshirt and folded it on top of the pizza box. He noticed a dark stain on the collar. He tried to wipe it away with his fingers and nails, but the stain wouldn't scratch off. It smelled like pizza sauce. Old people couldn't see or keep food on their plate. Maybe both things were related.

Hans went into the kitchen. He took the smoke detector off the wall and removed the battery. It beeped briefly before the red light faded. He lit his last cigarette in the bedroom.

His coughs didn't disturb Dal's sleep. She had a nice boat that was worth a lot of money. It was rusting in her driveway. It needed to be protected and then sold to someone who could use it. Hans thought maybe he could use it. He needed to learn how to swim first. He imagined himself in a white sailor's outfit on the boat with Dal by his side. Her age wouldn't matter as much on the open waters. He grabbed Dal's sweatshirt again. He put the cigarette out on the saucy stain until the cotton burned. A small hole with charred edges formed on the collar.

Neelam would know what to do with her mother. She always knew what to do in a crisis. She advised him not to smoke cigarettes with coffee after a late-night panic attack. The mix of caffeine and nicotine never overwhelmed his heart again. She was also responsible for curtailing his drinking, vacuuming his apartment, and getting his taxi washed every day, insisting that a cleaner car would lead to more customers and higher tips. He'd done these things for her as much as he'd done them with her.

Hans recited Neelam's phone number in his head. He put his face to the wall he shared with his neighbor, Greg. A music video was playing on the television. Hans walked outside into the freezing night and knocked on his door. Greg answered in a tank top, shorts, and a beer in his hand.

"I need to use your phone again," Hans said.

"I heard you in there with another woman," Greg said, as he took a sip from the can.

Hans stormed past him into his living room and picked up the phone by the television. "Can you turn the music down?" he said.

"She's a heavy walker."

"She's a little older."

"How much did she charge you?"

"She's not like the others," Hans said. "Can you turn off the television?" He started whispering the digits to himself as he clicked the buttons on the receiver. Greg went into the kitchen and came back with two beers.

"Do you want to share her tonight?" Greg asked. "I'll go fifty-fifty with you."

"It's not like that," Hans said.

The phone rang. He took a sip of the beer. Now was his chance to tell Neelam that he missed her and never should've left. He should've stopped drinking and smoking and fought for her. It would've been like a train station scene in a Bollywood epic. He attempted to leave town on the first train in the morning. Miraculously, Neelam snuck out of the lake house and followed him to the station, but her father and the neighborhood outlaws beat her there. Her father impeded her path and ordered the goons to pull her lover off the train and crush him on the rattling wooden planks, until finally the hero fought through the faceless bad guys and demanded that the father hand over his daughter to him honorably. Hans and Neelam then boarded the train together and disappeared to a remote mountain town in song.

"Hello?" Neelam said, through the phone.

Her sleepy voice instantly bound Hans in their past rhythms. She was a light sleeper and hated being woken up.

"Who is this?" she said.

"It's me," Hans said.

"Hans?"

"You remember me."

"It's the middle of the night."

"I was thinking about you," Hans said. "And your mother."

"Why were you thinking about my mother?"

"Have you thought about me?"

"How much have you had to drink?"

The same question she always asked him. His emotions were always filtered through the mask of intoxication. She still didn't take his feelings seriously. She hadn't changed. Hans didn't think he could change for her either. People didn't change. Hans took a large swig of his beer and hung up the phone.

"None of my business but what was that all about?" Greg said. He was sprawled on the couch now with a half-lit cigarette in his mouth.

"Family stuff," Hans said. "How much do I owe you for the call?"

"This one is on me," Greg said. "Go home to your girl."

Defeated, drunk, and smelling like cigarettes, Hans returned to his apartment and nestled beside Dal again.

Dal shivered upon his touch and shifted to accommodate his presence. "You remind me of back home," she said.

"Where?" Hans said. "You're having a nightmare." He inched closer to her, so their backs touched. His breaths quickly matched the rhythm of her heaving chest. "Do you still want a cigarette?"

"I don't smoke," Dal said. "You shouldn't either."

THE ASTROLOGER

Hans circled the block before stopping the taxi in the center of an intersection. Exasperated, he turned to his sister. "Which house is it?" he said.

"You should remember," Aarti said.

"You visit him every month," Hans said.

"He usually comes to my place."

"That would've been easier for me."

"You have patience for the entire world, but no time for me."

"Thursday is a busy taxi day. Everyone is coming and going."

"You've wasted forty years of Thursdays alone," she said. "This is your last chance to get help from the astrologer."

Hans had last visited the astrologer decades ago, when he'd struggled in high school. School was important in America, but English was a hard language to learn. The misshapen letters were difficult to write. The words never sounded exactly how they looked. Meaning was remote and absent.

According to Aarti, an astrologer was like a doctor who diagnosed the future. She believed the astrologer could help Hans improve his English. The astrologer recommended donating something yellow to someone in need. That would boost his studies. Hans donated bananas to the homeless man who hovered around the bleachers at school. It didn't help. He dropped out of high school a month after his last visit to the astrologer.

"Why do you still believe in all this?" Hans said.

"It's time for you to find a wife," Aarti said. "I'm almost sixty now. I'm not going to be around forever to take care of you."

"The astrologer has no control over that."

"You don't believe in anything," she said. "Nothing good will happen until you start believing."

"He's not married either."

"The astrologer is a man of God. Like me, he's beyond these worldly things."

"Then why do I have to get married?"

"The astrologer doesn't want to be with the outside world. He's deep into meditation like I am."

"Where's his house?" Hans said.

"You think I'm nobody. You don't even know my level," Aarti said. "Only the astrologer understands."

Hans continued driving in circles. He knew Aarti cared for him, but his misfortune was her purpose. He was an object of her faith and he used that to draw her attention. Sometimes it was a few dollars, a nice meal, or a place to sleep for a few nights. He could make a bigger ask from her if he played along with the astrologer. Maybe a new winter jacket or stereo for the taxi. He didn't feel bad about these transactions. Receiving favors in exchange for affirming Aarti's galactic faith wasn't manipulation. It was commerce.

"Do you have any specific questions for the astrologer?" Aarti said.

"We're never going to find him."

"I'm paying him a lot of money to help, but you're putting no effort into your own life."

Hans could use this money in better ways. The rusted rims of his taxi needed to be replaced. Without air fresheners, the car smelled like rotting fast food. Customers fixated on the ripped leather in the backseat. The brakes could last a little longer if he continued rolling through stop signs and traffic lights. A car wash. He'd quit smoking but would love to start again if he had the extra money. He couldn't tell Aarti about these earthly problems. She would pretend to be above his immediate needs and blame him for "thinking too small." Her head was lodged in the galaxies. She credited the position of the planets for his misfortunes, rather than the smell and appearance of his taxi.

"Keep circling the block," Aarti said. "Do you have a map?"
"Do you have the address?" Hans said.
"What kind of taxi driver doesn't carry a map?"
"I don't need help."
"Then why can't you find the house?"
"Is there anything I can do to make you happy?"
"You can become more like the astrologer."
"What's so special about him?"
"He respects God's planetary rules," Aarti said. "He's my spiritual guide."
"I don't need a guide," Hans said.
"Ask the astrologer about your birth chart," Aarti said. "That's the map of your life as prescribed by the planets. You should always keep it with you."

This was a pointless excursion. Hans was doing fine. He drove the taxi during the day and delivered pizzas at night. Car work suited him. After Neelam, he found love on odd nights. It was inconsistent and often nameless. Sometimes larger and older than he preferred and other times too scrawny and lifeless. He made enough in tips at both jobs to pay for it when he really needed it. He knew Aarti didn't care for love. She only wanted marriage, whereas he preferred the loneliness, frozen food, and company of his thoughts.

"How long will you keep doing this dirty work?" Aarti said.
"I like driving my taxi," Hans said. "I meet a lot of people."

"Probably all white people. Nobody you can marry."

"Everyone thinks I'm a nice person, except you."

"They must like pizza sauce because that's what all your clothes smell like."

"How can I be better for you?"

"By believing the astrologer."

"I don't understand his ways."

"There's no trust in your heart for anybody," Aarti said. "You have to surrender to him."

It started snowing as Hans turned into another cul-de-sac. A shirtless man pulled a trash bin to the end of his driveway. His legs were wrapped in a white sheet that he clutched with each awkward step. The man finished his cigarette, put it out under his bare foot and placed it in the trash. He leaned into the bin and emerged with a lighter. The sparks eventually flickered into a flame. He tucked the lighter into the white sheet and waddled up the driveway on his toes.

Hans laughed at the man's hunchback posture and uneven walk. His hips and arms swayed aggressively. He looked like a cartoon character stuck in the real world. "Trust him?" he said.

"The man searching through the garbage?" Aarti said.

"That's your astrologer, isn't it?"

"He must have accidentally thrown out something valuable."

Hans parked on the road beside the trash bin. His sister was a unique religious personality, so entrenched in a higher being, so supremely confident in God's existence and blessings that she didn't believe in negativity, despite all the bad things surrounding her. According to her, the saintly astrologer rummaging through garbage was probably part of God's plan, predetermined in the stars.

"Make sure you step outside with your right foot first," Aarti said. "You always step with your left foot first and that's wrong."

"Why would God care about these things?" Hans said.
"These are God's rules. Ask the astrologer about them."
"I don't need these answers."
"Do you have money to give him?"
"You're paying him enough already."

Aarti dug into her oversized purse. "The astrologer is a messenger of God," she said. "Giving money to him is the same as giving to God." She handed Hans a ten-dollar bill. "Place this at his feet when you go inside."

Hans gladly took the money. He followed Aarti up the driveway as they walked to the side of the house. The snowy path was stained with cigarette butts. Aarti knocked on the side door. The astrologer answered in the same white sheet, or *dhoti*, still shirtless, but now with a long white scarf wrapped loosely around his neck which barely hid his enormous belly. The sloppy red and yellow markings on his forehead reeked of religious intentions. His bushy mustache blended with his nose hairs. His head bobbed slightly to the right when he smiled.

"It's an auspicious time to arrive," the astrologer said. "The stars are in your favor today."

Aarti leaned forward and grazed the astrologer's feet with her hands before bringing them to her heart, a gesture he accepted by placing his palm on her forehead. Hans opted for a distant wave, but the astrologer was eager to provide blessings. He stepped toward Hans and needlessly placed his hand on his scalp. The astrologer smelled like chewing tobacco.

"You are so busy," Aarti said. "We are blessed to have some of your time today."

"The pleasure is mine," the astrologer said. "I prepared our materials downstairs in the prayer room."

Aarti covered her head with her transparent scarf as they descended the stairs to the basement, past a metallic sculpture of the sleepy-eyed elephant God. The basement had the pungent odor of a dingy underground cellar masked with copious amounts of incense. The result was more nauseating than divine. An electric stovetop and mini refrigerator sat on a foldable table. Used paper plates were stained the same yellow color as the wall above the stovetops. They stepped around two rusty chairs. The ceiling got lower. Hans heard the water flowing through the pipes after a flush by the tenants upstairs. The lone bedroom in the basement was the designated meeting room. Colorful images of deities decorated a makeshift bookshelf. Christmas lights accented the photo frames. The three of them sat cross-legged on the cold basement floor. The astrologer reached into his *dhoti* and pulled out a lighter. He lit the flame and applied it to three sticks of incense underneath his homemade altar. The incense smoke clouded the damp basement air.

"Your friend Bindu came to see me yesterday," the astrologer said. "I'm so sorry about her husband."

"He died during a good time," Aarti said. "January is a good time to die."

"The planets guide us but sometimes there are unforeseen occurrences that can't be accounted for," the astrologer said.

"He had cancer," Hans said.

"But his thoughts were always negative," Aarti said. "You have to think positive."

"Thinking positive could cure cancer?"

"He knew he would die."

"How did he know?"

Aarti turned to the astrologer. "He was enlightened like you."

"Then how did he get cancer?" Hans said.

"He went months without talking to Bindu."

"Why?"

"Like me, he didn't want to be with the outside world," Aarti said. "He was deep into meditation like I am."

Hans turned to the astrologer. "Is this true?"

"These are the mysteries of the universe," the astrologer said. "Anything is possible."

Hans put his head down and smiled in appreciation of Aarti's absurd religious performance. According to his sister, Bindu's husband was nothing but a weak lump of negative thoughts. If positive thinking could cure cancer, then maybe it could help Hans earn more tips.

"You think this is funny?" Aarti said.

"I was thinking about Bindu Aunty," Hans said. "She's nice. She deserves better."

"Today we're worried about you."

The astrologer took Aarti's cue and rearranged the stainless steel plate, glasses, and bowls on the basement floor. He centered the dishware between Hans and himself. The plate contained pink petals, unground black peppers, and a glass of cloudy water. "Do you understand what we're doing here today?"

"Something to help me," Hans said.

"We are making an offering to your fallen ancestors," the astrologer said. "Requesting their help to find you a suitable wife."

Hans lingered on "suitable." Who was the right woman for him? Cooking ability was essential. Thin but not too thin. Maybe thin with shape. He liked it when women wore long boots, the ones that came up to their knees and almost touched their short leather skirts. She had to be a good swimmer or at least look comfortable in a swimsuit like the girls in car magazines. But she couldn't be seen like that in public. His taxi was the only car she could pose with. She had to be younger. Women his age didn't look good in swimming clothes. She had to abstain from alcohol but tolerate his drinking. What if God was real? It was best to be safe in case astrology was also true. He needed someone who believed in the divine so she could pray for both of them, just in case.

"Will it take long?" Hans said. "My taxi shift starts soon."

"The movement of the planets can't be rushed," the astrologer said.

Hans moved his hands above the plate while the astrologer placed petals and peppers in his hand and poured water over the mixture. It had an intoxicating odor, like cheap vodka. As instructed, Hans leaned his fingers forward to let the liquid drip into the plate. Other times he angled his hands so the water slipped between his thumb and index finger to create a small stream that splashed on the plate. The astrologer recited indistinguishable sentences in an ancient tongue. The consistency in his motion could only be achieved through years of repetition and rehearsal.

"Now, I want you to drink this next offering," the astrologer said.

Hans formed a bowl with his hands and placed it close to his mouth as the astrologer poured the cloudy liquid. He slurped it as the astrologer kept pouring. It wasn't water. It was vodka. The astrologer winked at Hans. He dumped more into his hands until Hans coughed and pushed the astrologer away. The vodka dripped down his face and onto his shirt.

"You can't even do the ritual right," Aarti said. "You made a mess of the holy water."

The astrologer winked at Hans again and handed him a damp cloth that did little to dry his hands or shirt.

"The water didn't taste holy," Hans said.

"Not to worry," the astrologer said. "As his conduit to the planets, I'll finish it for him to save the ritual." He raised the glass to his mouth and swallowed the remaining vodka.

Hans's head spun. He enjoyed vodka but it had been too much, too fast. The scope of the galaxy must only have been comprehensible through intoxication.

The ritual woke up Aarti, who appeared to be the first to benefit from the prayers and offerings of wet petals. "Nothing is happening for Hans," she said. "Nothing is going as we had hoped."

The astrologer reached for his notebook and scrolled through pages of illegible symbols, charts, and squares before landing on a page that had Hans's first name, birth date, and time of birth printed in the top right corner. In the center of the page was a square divided into twelve segments, some of them blank, others crowded with odd characters.

Hans suddenly feared the astrologer's powers. What if he could really read his life? Did he know that Hans masturbated to smiles in dentist advertisements? He'd once argued with a deaf girl at the bar when she didn't hear his advances. He never flushed in public bathrooms or paid taxes. He'd once stolen a child's jacket during a taxi ride because he liked its smoky smell. Another time, he upset an Indian customer because of his Christian name, John. Hans berated him for being a traitor to his people and religion. Did the astrologer share Hans's secrets with Aarti? She might have learned some things when she did his laundry every Sunday. The stains and smells were obvious, but there was no way she could discern the details without the astrologer's help. There had to be a standard of confidentiality between the astrologer and his patrons, like doctors with their patients and Hans with his taxi customers. It was an unwritten code of silence. What happened in the backseat was never repeated.

"As I said in our previous meetings, your brother was born at an auspicious time. I have yet to see a birth chart of such magnitude and prowess," the astrologer said.

Hans glanced up, expecting to see the planets rotating above their heads, but there was only a crack in the discolored ceiling protruding from the tube light.

"According to his birth chart, he would do best with water-based work. That includes gas stations and liquor stores where fluids flow. What is the nature of your current work?"

"I drive a taxi," Hans said. "And deliver pizzas."

The astrologer scribbled a few lines adjacent to the square. The birth chart evolved into a three-dimensional diagram where the lines and shapes appeared to move tangentially off the page. Hans looked away to calm his spinning thoughts.

"That's wonderful too," the astrologer said. "The color yellow is lucky for you."

"I will buy him a yellow sweater," Aarti said.

The taxi had been lucky for Hans a few times. It was mostly a cash business and helped him find love. He used to like college girls the best. They had so much money that they sometimes forgot to carry enough with them. But they always made up for it in other ways. He thought it was fair. Good business. An exchange of transportation for pleasure.

"Despite the strength of his birth chart, nobody lives a perfect life," the astrologer said. "I can perform a more detailed analysis if you have specific questions."

"Marriage is the most important thing," Aarti said. "When will he get married?"

"Life in our culture begins at marriage," the astrologer said. "Do you have someone in your life? We can help arrange the wedding."

Hans had difficulty remaining upright. His legs had fallen asleep. He swayed in every direction. "I feel sick," he said.

"That is the power of the ritual," Aarti said.

"My eyes are burning."

"The planets are showing us their powers," the astrologer said.

Hans felt himself sweating through his clothes. The repulsion of his own odor made him gag. His throat and abdomen burned. Vodka always did this to him. The astrologer probably knew that too.

The astrologer turned to Aarti. "Why don't we do the ritual again to make sure it worked," he said. "This time we'll do it with you. Hans will get double the benefits."

"That would be delightful," Aarti said. "I will wash my hands and feet first."

Aarti left the room. Moments later, Hans heard water running in the tub. Hans's intoxication increased the frequency of the astrologer's smiles. His winks morphed into twitches. The vodka had gone straight to Hans's eyes and blurred his vision.

"Will this cost extra?" Hans said.

"Time is money in any country," the astrologer said.

Hans regretted not leaving his taxi meter on. The glowing red numbers on the dashboard represented the cost of this visit and the worth of his own time. Aarti needed to see those escalating dollar figures so she would finally appreciate his work.

"Now, tell me the truth," the astrologer said. "How many white girls have you been with?"

"What?" Hans said.

"Oh, come on, you have your own car. A money-minded gentleman like you has probably been with many girls."

"I've been with some," Hans said, counting on one hand.

"They are so delightful, if you know what I mean."

"What was in that drink?"

"You liked it?"

"It's stronger than anything I've ever had in this world," Hans said.

"When I was young like you, I'd go to a bar every weekend to do palm readings," the astrologer said. "I had them eating out of my hand, if you know what I mean."

"Holy men aren't supposed to visit unholy places."

"You should marry Bindu. Older women are the best, if you know what I mean."

"She's like an aunt to me."

"But not really your aunt."

"What did you do to her yesterday?"

"There are rituals only performed privately after drinking the holy water, if you know what I mean."

"I don't want to know what you mean."

"Okay, you don't have to marry her, but take a turn. Widows are carefree. Nobody is looking over their shoulder anymore."

The thought of his drunk aunt being consumed by this disgusting man briefly sobered Hans. The astrologer posturing as a humble servant of the planets was as false as the hope he promised. "What about my life?" Hans said. "And all the drawings in your notebook?"

The astrologer handed Hans the notebook. "Take a look," he said. "It's all bullshit, if you know what I mean."

The curse word sounded more foreign than the syllables of incomprehensible prayers that had echoed from the astrologer's mouth earlier. It didn't suit his native dress and appearance.

"I knew you couldn't help me find a wife," Hans said.

"You don't need these superstitions in America," the astrologer said. "Here we have choices. It's not like back home where people live on hope alone. We have opportunities here. There's women living free everywhere here."

Hans tried deciphering the symbols, arrows, and text on the page. It was more intimidating than English. He recognized his birthday and time of birth. Everything else was a lie. It didn't matter how many bananas he donated or how much yellow he wore. His skepticism was confirmed. The planets didn't care about his existence. The only truth was the life he'd lived and would keep living alone.

"Sometimes parents bring me their teenage daughters because they're trying to get into the top colleges, if you know what I mean," the astrologer said.

"You're a criminal," Hans said.

"It's not a crime to enjoy women."

"Poisoning kids is a crime."

The astrologer refilled the glass and took another sip. "It's holy water. It arouses the planets and our senses. It gives them hope."

"You're sick."

"This is how I learned to do my job back home," the astrologer said. "The planets made me this way."

"This isn't how they do things in this country."

"You think you're better than me just because you drive a taxi? We're both in the cash business. I bet you don't pay any taxes either. We could disappear today and the American government wouldn't notice."

"I'm nothing like you."

"Godless people like you always think you're better than us."

"I've never hurt anybody."

"Your sister seems to be in a lot of pain over your failings."

Hans remembered the gun in his glove compartment. "I'll kill you," he said.

"You came here for advice," the astrologer said. "I'm giving it to you. Enjoy your life like me."

Aarti returned to the room and noticed the notebook in Hans's lap.

"You're learning astrology now?" she said. "That's wonderful. You're becoming a holy man like our astrologer."

"He is a fast learner," the astrologer said.

"Can you teach him how to read palms? Like you used to read mine."

Hans lifted the notebook over his head. "This is all nonsense. This man is a sinner."

Aarti slapped Hans across the face. "God sent him here to help us."

"I'm trying to protect you," Hans said.

"You can help me by listening to his holy advice," Aarti said. "Help me by letting him help you."

"He's dangerous."

"Then I wish you were dangerous. I wish you were more like him."

"How can you believe him over me?"

"Because he's everything to me," Aarti said.

The astrologer watched the argument with a crooked smile. Hans wanted to pass his sister's slap forward to the astrologer. What did "everything" mean? Were they lovers? Is that why the astrologer visited Aarti at her place? His sister was a willing victim. Hans cringed at the thought of her engaging in disgusting pleasures with this grotesque liar. The planets were an excuse for dirty tricks. It was easier to strip after consuming the holy water. It warmed your body from the inside. It hurt Hans more to think about the helpless teenagers. If their God wasn't going to help, then maybe he had to do something.

"I'm going to call the police," Hans said.

The astrologer maintained an erect posture and steadied his eyes, instantly returning to his reverent form. "The poor child is mistaken and confused," he said.

"Tell her what you asked me," Hans said. "And tell her what you did with Bindu."

"All he asked was if there's someone in your life who we should know about," Aarti said.

The astrologer cleared his throat. "The truth is that Hans confessed to me. He told me about a white woman in his life."

"That can't be true," Aarti said. "He would never betray me like that."

Hans clutched the astrologer's notebook. He pointed it at him. "He's a dirty liar," he said.

"I dreamed about being a great sister-in-law," Aarti said. "I was going to be the best, but now I can't. I would give your wife everything. Now you've left me with nothing."

"White women are very nice people," the astrologer said. "But in our culture, for marriage, Indians are best."

"Hans doesn't follow anything," Aarti said. "He thinks he's special but there's nothing special about him. He doesn't deserve a nice Indian wife."

Aarti was right. Hans was lucky to have made it this far from their small Indian village. He had his own taxi. It was an honest livelihood. Hans wasn't special. But he was sure that he was a better man than the astrologer. He never used his job to take advantage of women or mock others. Aarti had to know that he was a good person.

Hans ripped the page with his birth chart out of the notebook and crunched it in his fist. He tapped the astrologer's shoulder. "Give me the lighter," he said.

The astrologer's bushy unibrow shifted synchronously with his mustache. "I only have knowledge of the planets to impart," he said.

Hans tackled the astrologer. They both tipped over to their sides. Hans snatched one end of his *dhoti* and pulled until it unraveled. The astrologer screamed and clutched at the cloth, desperately trying to keep himself covered.

Aarti grabbed Hans's shoulder. "You're hurting him," she said. "Leave him alone."

"God is watching," the astrologer said.

"I hope so," Hans said, as he tugged harder at the cloth. Each pull turned the astrologer to his side. The further he spun away, the more naked he became. The hair on his lower back stretched into his stained underwear. The astrologer turned, sat upright, and crossed his arms over his midsection. Aarti turned the other way.

"You can look," Hans said. "He's a normal disgusting man."

"God will punish you for this," Aarti said. She removed her head scarf and covered the astrologer with it. He wrapped it around his waist like a skirt.

Hans searched the pile of white cloth until he found the lighter. He unwrinkled the notebook page and turned to his sister. "It doesn't matter what's written here," he said. "I'm not a bad person."

"You could be good if you followed something," Aarti said. "You can start today."

Hans brought the page closer to the flame. "Nothing will ever be enough for you," he said.

"I'm all you have," Aarti said. "You will die alone if you burn that sacred map."

The idea of being old and lonely with only his thoughts as company amused Hans. It wouldn't be much different than his life so far.

The flame flickered. Aarti threw the glass of remaining holy water at Hans. The vodka dripped down his face. It stung his eyes as a flash lit the room.

Hans wiped his face. The flame caught the drops of vodka on the back of his hand, instantly burning the hairs on his wrist. The fire climbed up his arm as fast as the meter ticked up in his taxi.

Aarti shielded herself from the fire. "See," she said. "The holy water cursed you."

ACKNOWLEDGMENTS

Gratefully acknowledged are the following publications, where stories first appeared:

"Gatsby": *Puerto del Sol*

"Taxi": *Midwest Review*; selected for the *Best Debut Short Stories 2021: The PEN American Dau Prize*

"Stranded in the Dunes": *Southern Humanities Review*

"Dinner Party": *Great River Review*

"Tony and Jim's": *Southern Humanities Review*

* * *

It's Thanksgiving 2019 in Las Cruces, New Mexico. We're hosting a misfit group of graduate students and family at our apartment to celebrate the holiday. We've eaten, had dessert, plenty of wine, and even played some card games. Inevitably, our conversation turns to reading and writing. Somehow, and I don't even remember how, my dear friend Tim Loperfido is holding a Raymond Carver anthology. Tim flips to the story "Popular Mechanics." He reads it out loud to a captive and tipsy audience. I remember thinking, "Wow, this is a writer's life." Much love to Tim for an impromptu life-changing public reading and agonizing over these stories with me line-by-line, over and over again. Thank you for helping me fall in love with the writing process.

Most of these stories were written during Covid. Infinite love to the Pool Prodigies Covid bubble—Ethi House, Eric House, and Holly Brause—for keeping me sane in the most insane circumstances.

Let's go further back to 2007. I'm a reporter at a weekly newspaper in Flint, Michigan. I'm writing community news, spending my days recapping local city council and school board meetings with a new business profile sprinkled in. I stayed late one night to finish my story on the expansion of a local cemetery. It's just the sports editor, Patrick Hayes, and I in the newsroom. We started talking sports. At one point, one of us said, "Do you read Deadspin?" And that was the beginning of our lifelong best friendship and bromance. Patty, thank you for being the first editor who believed in me as a writer. You gave me the freedom and independence to write what I wanted, trust my instincts, and screw the word count limits. I wish we were still working super late on Friday nights with the Carmelo Anthony and Allen Iverson Denver Nuggets on in the background.

Fast forward to 2009 when I met Rus Bradburd at his book signing at a Tulsa University basketball game. Rus and I connected over our love for basketball. I also told him I was interested in writing fiction. Rus immediately engaged in my interest, treated me like a fiction writer even though I had yet to complete a story, and barely had any ideas. He even agreed to read my horrible first drafts. And he's read every single thing I've written since. Rus, you've been a great mentor and dear friend. This book wouldn't have been possible without you. Thank you for investing in me as a writer and person. Your kindness and humanity permeate every page of this book.

I also became a groupie in 2009. Weary- and teary-eyed after teaching elementary school all day, I ran into Aaron

Tinjum in the hallway of our apartment building. Aaron carried a guitar in a hard case in one hand and dragged a amp-speaker on wheels in the other.

"Where are you going?" I asked.

"Do you want to come to a rock and roll show?" Aaron said.

"Sure."

"You take the amp."

Aaron handed me the amp. It was heavy! And that was our origin story. I watched him play a show at the Gypsy Cafe and we have since traveled the world together. Thank you for believing in your art and mine. I'll always drag that amp across the broken Tulsa sidewalks for you. In some ways, I still am.

A huge shout out to all the journals that individually published these stories and the many cohorts at New Mexico State University that read and provided invaluable feedback. A part of all of you exists in these stories. Ditto with the Flint Journal PD's crew and Enso's Tulsa Charter Corps.

Brandon Hobson—thank you for challenging convention in my writing, pushing me to read more, and humanizing the writing process. You've never hesitated to share your experiences, network, and sports picks with me. I'm forever thankful for that. You're always right about the writing, but rarely about the sports.

We're moving up to 2014 now. I'm working at a small engineering college with Kenneth Zahrt. I've heard from other co-workers that Ken is a fiction writer too. I finally meet him at a fireside chat with the president of the college. We stand together as we listen to admissions trends in higher education. Boring. We start talking but I can't get over the fact that he's my age and bald because I'm balding as well. There's a big bald spot in the back of my head. Before we ever talked about reading and writing, I point to my bald spot and ask him, "Is this how it started for you?" At first he ignores my question, but then finally says, "Are you seriously asking me that?" Believe it or not, that was the start of our writing journey together. Kenneth, thank you for talking out all these stories with me and telling me to go for it.

Nana Kwame Adjei-Brenyah—you once told me that I was "not afraid to be me." Thank you for championing my work and writing style.

Maria Kuznetsova—thank you for finding the humor in my writing.

Anna Qu—thank you for understanding what an immigrant experience is and never shying away from talking about it in-person and on the page.

Hasreet—thank you for a beautiful cover design. I couldn't have asked for a better artistic partner. I'm inspired by your art and am so thankful that you'll always be creatively tied to this book.

Oliver—thank you for consulting on the cover design and gracefully absorbing my hilarious jokes at your expense. Next cover design is all you so get back in the studio and get better every day.

The one person who has read this book more times than me is my younger sister Shana. I hated most of her edits but she was right half the time, maybe just a quarter of the time. I hate it when she's right. Let me say it here once and for all. You were right about some things! Not all, but some, not as many as you think. You were the first person to encourage me to write fiction, first person to ever read it, and the first person to call Hans "disgusting."

Mother—you drive me crazy but you're essential to this writing journey. I know what I've written is passable if it makes you mad. I know it's really good if it makes you furious. Thank you for being my support and barometer.

Dad—I wish you were here to see the life we've built.

Publishing a book has been my dream for as long as I can remember. To publisher Dr. Ross Tangedal, editor Brett Hill, the sales/media team of Sophie McPherson and Sam

Bjork, and all the staff at Cornerstone Press—thank you for making my dream come true!

We're almost at the end now. Hang in there with me.

One more fast forward to 2018. I'm working for the State of Michigan and Rus is inviting me to come study with him in New Mexico. I jokingly tell my partner Sara about the invite.

"I said no."

"Why did you say no?" Sara said.

"Because I have a good full-time job. We could buy a house soon."

"But don't you want to write?"

"Yes."

"Then why don't we go?"

"I don't know."

"Call him back."

I did call him back. We left everything we'd built together in Michigan to take a chance on my writing in New Mexico. I'm not much of a risk-taker myself. But, Sara, you've inspired me to take chances on myself, our family, and our life together. You make me a better writer and person. And you're not afraid to tell me to "cut it out" when my neuroses takes over logic. Thank you for always being there for me. You make me happy every single day.

To Milo and Rio—I hope you avoid the trauma that inspired the characters in this collection, but I also hope you get some of the chaos of an immigrant family full of drunk uncles hiding things in the glove compartments of their car. Also, you're too young to read these stories. Put this book down. You have to wait until you are 18. Sorry, make that 35. Everything I do is for both of you.

PARDEEP TOOR is the winner of the PEN American Dau Prize, and his writing has appeared in the *Best Debut Short Stories 2021, Southern Humanities Review, Electric Literature, Midwest Review,* and *Longreads*. He grew up in Brampton, Ontario, and currently lives in Colorado.

www.ingramcontent.com/pod-product-compliance
Lightning Source LLC
LaVergne TN
LVHW040105080526
838202LV00045B/3788